Seeking the White Root

An Australian Story

Cinda Wombles Pettigrew
and
Robyn D. Warner

Bald Eagle Press

Seeking the White Root is a work of fiction. Names, characters, places, and incidents are the product of the author's imagination or are used fictitiously. Any resemblance to actual events, locales, or persons, living or dead, is entirely coincidental.

2nd Printing, 1999
Copyright 1998 by Cinda Wombles Pettigrew
All rights reserved
Printed in U.S.A.
Library of Congress Catalog 98-72444
ISBN 0-9666739-0-5

Cover design by Richard Ferguson
Text design by Sheryl Mehary

Bald Eagle Press
P.O. Box 422
Louisiana, Missouri 63353

Dedicated to the stolen genera-
tion – the multitude of Aboriginal
children that were taken from their
parents, "for their welfare," by white
"Protection and Welfare Societies" –
that their wounds may heal.

ⓑ ⓑ ⓑ

A portion of the proceeds from
the sale of Seeking the White Root will
be donated to an organization
dedicated to providing assistance to
re-uniting the "stolen generation"
with their Aboriginal families.

Acknowledgments

We, the authors wish to express our gratitude to:

... our husbands, Jim Pettigrew and Peter Newall, for their love and continuing support, without which this work may not have been completed.

... our wonderful families, for their encouragement.

... Hazel, for helping to save the rainforest, by teaching others to see it through her sensitive eyes.

... Ray and Jacinta King, for their friendship and for introducing us to each other.

... all the teachers and friends who assisted us at different times on our individual spiritual journeys.

... *Team Destiny,* for their friendship and encouragement.

... Holly Tiendi Newall, for blessing us with her recent arrival in our lives, may her generation know the true meaning of equality.

Table of Contents

Foreword

As two women who only see the world through white eyes, in no way do we claim to know what it means to be Aboriginal. The actions, descriptions, language and feelings of the Aboriginal characters depicted in this book are for the most part constructed from the authors' imaginations. There is nothing in our backgrounds to suggest an intimate knowledge of Aboriginal ways or beliefs. However, we both strongly believe that, if one viewed the world as a classroom with an Aboriginal teacher, the emphasis of the curriculum would be on nature, community, ceremony and spirituality. If we all were to graduate, the quality of life would be tremendously enhanced.

Article from the *Minneapolis Star Tribune*, 1997
Associated Press

Unofficial apology offered to Aborigines

Premier is first to express regrets over adoption policy

MELBOURNE, AUSTRALIA – A policy that sought to "save" Aborigine children by forcibly taking them from their parents spawned lasting trauma and resulted in a "stolen generation," Australia's premier said Monday in an apology.

John Howard offered his regrets personally, not on behalf of the government, for the policy that removed an estimated 100,000 children from their parents between 1910 and the early 1970s in the belief that the Aborigines were a doomed race.

Light-skinned children were given to white families for adoption. Dark-skinned children were put in orphanages.

"Personally, I feel deep sorrow for those of my fellow Australians who suffered under the practices of past generation towards indigenous people," Howard told delegates at the Australian Reconciliation Convention.

Howard's apology drew strong applause at first from the nearly 2,000 delegates. But many booed and shouted when he said, "Australians of this generation shouldn't be required to accept guilt and blame for past actions and policy over which they had no control."

A number of Australia's whites believe they have no reason to apologize for past wrong-doing. Others say a heartfelt general apology is warranted, along with compensation.

A report issued Monday by a federal human rights commission recommends that Australia's governments set up

---

⚘ X ⚘

a fund to compensate victims of the adoption policy. The federal government has said it will reject the idea.

It also rejects the report's assertion that the adoption policy could be considered a form of genocide as defined by a 1946 U.N. resolution.

Australia's 303,000 Aborigines, who were given full citizenship in May, 1967, lag behind other Australians in access to jobs, education and health services.

Prologue

Mid 1800s
Off the Southern Coast of Victoria
Australia

ⓖ   ⓖ   ⓖ

The sea was very dark today. An eerie calm encompassed the ship. Joanna sat staring, straining to see past the waves to the horizon, looking for land. They should be very close now. The journey had been long and hard and all aboard were anxious to reach their destination. Joanna was sitting in her favorite spot on the bowsprit. She had to be careful not to let her mother see her or she'd be in trouble. Her mother thought it was much too dangerous, that she would slip and fall through the ropes. Not so, Joanna felt quite secure here, enveloped by the huge knots of thick rope. This was her spot, Joanna had decided, because it was her ship. Had not her father, the ship's captain, named the ship, *The Joanna,* for her? She was extremely proud to be sailing toward her new home on her own ship.

She often daydreamed about the day they would arrive in the new country. There would be lots of people at the port eagerly awaiting their arrival. *The Joanna* was a famous ship on its second voyage and people would be excited by the prospect of news from their homeland. The ship was stocked with a cargo of goods not readily available in the new land, which her father planned to sell when he arrived. Joanna wondered what her new home would be like and if she would have many friends. The voyage had been rather lonely, as there were few other children on board and none her age. The adults hadn't been much fun; many had been sick most of the way. Joanna was never sick and she pretty much had the run of the ship except when her mother felt well enough to come looking for her. Joanna hid from her as much as possible. It was much more fun to tie knots with the sailors and listen to their tales of distant lands, than doing cross stitch next to her mother's bed as her mother lay moaning, suffering from the constant rocking motion of the waves.

As Joanna sat staring at the horizon, she suddenly realized the sky had darkened and she could scarcely see the difference between sky and sea. She heard the sailor from the lookout cry the warning of a storm approaching. "All hands on deck! Batten down the hatches!" Joanna scrambled off the bowsprit. She knew better than to try to ride out the storm from there. The sea was turning rough quickly, and the wind was tearing through the sails. Everyone dashed about, shouting, and Joanna became frightened. Other storms had not seemed this scary. She hurried toward her parents' cabin slipping and falling as waves crashed over the bow. The cry, "Land Ho!" sounded and she was totally engulfed by water at the same moment.

When Joanna awoke, she was curled up in a little ball in someone's arms. She looked up, expecting to see her mother, and was startled to see a strange black face. She struggled to free herself and felt a sharp, shooting pain in her hip. The voice of the woman holding her was soothing, but Joanna could not understand her words. The woman's embrace felt warm and strong and Joanna calmed as she filled with a sense of security. Joanna looked around and realized they were on a sand dune overlooking a beach. She tried again to sit up, her hip collapsed and she cried out in pain. The black woman assisted her, supporting her hip so it didn't hurt so much. Joanna looked down the beach which was covered with broken wood, trunks, and other objects not recognizable. In the distance, she could barely see her father and two black people dragging something, or someone, across the beach. Overcome by pain and emotion, Joanna fainted.

The Next Day ...

Nguyah watched the sky, as though it were still angry, burn a crimson dawn across the water even after it destroyed the ship. Gulls circled and swooped, searching through the wreckage of the broken ship for bits of food. Bodies of several men had been washed ashore and the beach had begun to stink. Nguyah observed that the big white man leading the survivors in the direction of the white settlement, wasn't very nice. He had spoken in a loud, harsh voice and roughly pushed Nguyah aside as he plucked the child from her arms. The child had screamed with pain. Nguyah wondered why the white man was so mean. She had given the child her breath back when she found her on the beach all twisted and broken, with seaweed in her mouth. Later Nguyah noticed that the only body the big white man buried, was that of a woman, probably the child's mother.

Nguyah glanced out over the beach and saw a large box. It did not appear broken as most everything else was. The men from her family were starting down to the beach, having already dug holes in the soft earth on the backside of the headland. They would bury the bodies in the holes, giving them back to the earth. Nguyah went down to the beach and took a closer look at the box. It was made from a wood with an intricate grain. It looked as though it would open on top, but Nguyah pried with her fingers along the crack near the top and nothing happened. It was just as well, whatever secrets it contained would remain there. Nguyah decided to take the box to the little girl. Perhaps the box had belonged to her mother. The child would surely be lonely without a mother in a strange land.

Some Time Later ...

Nguyah stood again on a hill overlooking the beach. She felt sad. She had come to say goodbye to the beach and the sea. Her family must move. She remembered the shipwreck and how much her people had tried to help the white survivors. Those white people were a strange tribe. They took everything and gave nothing back. They even claimed they owned the earth. Nobody can own the earth, not even if you call it "land." What a strange word for the earth.

Nguyah shook her head. It didn't matter what she thought. The big white man had destroyed everything. He said he owned all the land and then cut down all the beautiful old trees as Nguyah had watched sadly from the edge of the bush. He worked hard every day, never seeming to rest. Nguyah had often wondered when he had time for his children or for ceremonies. There was so much she had been curious about, wanting to know what the white man's customs were and why they did certain things.

There had not been any opportunity to learn. The big white man had banned the Aborigine from his farm because they had refused to help him cut the trees. Her people had stood and watched him for a couple of days, which had made him very angry. The white man hadn't even used much of the wood; instead he set fire to the remaining branches. He had split the trunks to build a house, and that was all right. But those beautiful big trees were the earth's gift to her people. They had given food, shelter and spiritual strength to Nguyah and her family and to all the creatures of the forest.

All the time he was cutting the trees, Nguyah had been unable to sleep at night hearing the animals and birds crying out because their homes were being destroyed. Many of the animals had actually burned to death in the raging fires he had started. Even the trees cried, their spirits moaning as they were dying. Now, there was no longer a forest, only bare earth, grass and long lonely hills dotted with the white man's sheep.

Nguyah and her people had been forced to move north to a dense rainforest area, as there was no food or shelter remaining. Nguyah had been deeply disappointed when they moved because she could no longer watch over Joanna every day. Joanna had never fully recovered from the traumatic shipwreck. Her hip had not healed correctly, and she walked with a limp. She had seemed so sad and lonely that Nguyah had often gone to the white settlement to visit. Nguyah wasn't allowed to be there so she had to hide in the bushes. She would mimic the sound of a honeyeater so Joanna would know she was there. Nguyah would watch Joanna's face light up when she heard the call. Joanna would make sure her father wasn't watching, and then follow the sound until she found Nguyah in the bushes.

Nguyah would give her a big hug and Joanna would snuggle down into the warmth of her lap and listen while Nguyah told her stories in a language she couldn't understand. Nguyah loved to stroke Joanna's fine blonde hair; it felt so different from her own. Unfortunately, one day Joanna's father had crept up on them in the bush. He had roared with anger, and brandishing a stick, he had advanced on Nguyah shouting for her to get out and never touch his daughter again. Joanna had cried and screamed at her father, but he had wrenched her arm violently and tightened his grip so she could not get away. Terrified, Nguyah had fled, running as fast as her feet could carry her. She never saw Joanna again. Nguyah never stopped asking the spirits in the skies to look after her beloved little blonde girl.

The elders had decided that the tribe had to move far away to find a new home. There would be a ceremony tomorrow night. A member of a nearby tribe had arrived in camp a few days ago and told them stories that made their hair stand on end. He said that seven days' walk along the coast from where they lived, there was a white settler who had invited many of his tribesmen in and had given them plates of porridge. They were grateful for the food, as the winter had been lean and hard. The white settler invited them to come back anytime. So one day, while some members of the tribe were out hunting, the ones who stayed behind went to the white settler's house seeking more food. He again fed them well but this time he had put poison in the food. They died, writhing on the ground. A fellow tribesman, returning from the hunt early, saw him pushing their limp bodies into a gaping hole. Nguyah and her tribe were horrified and frightened by the massacre. The council of elders met and it was decided that they must move away. Nguyah sighed as she took one last look at the sea, and started back to camp with a heavy heart. Her homeland had changed forever and she would never return.

Later, they had a big ceremony. They danced all the bird, animal, tree and plant dances and said farewell to the only home they'd known. All the tribe members vowed to return as soon as it was safe, but they knew in their hearts that their homeland would never be the same. The visiting tribesman, who had brought the ominous news, decided to stay with Nguyah's people since the remaining members of his tribe were now scattered. He had heard that many tribes were going to Gariwerd, the great mountains, to visit the cave of Bunjil. A special ceremony involving all the tribes was planned in order to ask Bunjil, their Creator, what they should do. So Nguyah's tribe packed their hunting sticks, grinding stones and gourds, and headed northwest. It was time to leave. Aboriginal people could not live the way of the white man for long without losing spirit. Without spirit, there is no real life.

Chapter One

The Sheep Station

⊚　　⊚　　⊚

A Century Later – The Australian Outback

It was evening and the scent of honeysuckle was strong here on the veranda just outside her bedroom. Mary gazed over the rolling hills. She could see the sheep dotting the long line of brown and blue on the horizon. There had been no rain for such an unbearably long time that her husband Rod was worried about the pasture. Scanning the sky furtively for clouds, she sighed. Would there ever be a break from this smothering heat? She admitted she felt stronger now. If only it would rain, then everything would be all right.

Six months had passed since Janey was born. She was such a big baby, making labor extremely difficult. If it hadn't been for Narana, Mary might not have survived. Rod had sent for the doctor, but he arrived two days after the birth. Although the doctor disdainfully pulled the smelly poultice of herbs and plants off Mary and threw it on the veranda, he couldn't explain why the bleeding had stopped. It was obvious she'd nearly bled to death. When Fiona had arrived from Melbourne two weeks later and heard the story, she thanked Narana personally for saving both her sister and her niece.

Narana had always seemed a little odd. She talked to herself constantly and had a peculiar scent about her. The smell reminded Mary of being beside a brook in a gully where the ferns grew dense, the water dripped off the trees, and one had to take care not to slide into the water when walking along the muddy bank. That was the smell Mary realized, mud. Narana smelled like the earth, musty and fresh at the same time.

Just then, Narana stepped out onto the veranda with Janey in her arms. "Do you want hold little Janna before she goes sleep?"

Mary nodded with a little smile as Narana tucked the baby in her arms and backed away. Tears trickled down Mary's cheeks and an overwhelming feeling of love swelled within her breast as she gazed down at the little blonde ringlets and looked deep into Janey's wide blue eyes. A lump rose in Mary's throat as the baby groped for her mother's breast. She felt so guilty. She hadn't been able to feed Janey since she became ill and her milk had dried up. Narana had been feeding Janey for the past week or so. "So what?" she told herself. The baby seemed happy and strong.

Narana was boiling all their water now. Rod also had been sick, but he wouldn't rest. He just kept pushing himself. Narana and the other murries, the name the

Aborigines called themselves, had been sick too, but they recovered quickly. Narana had offered Mary and Rod what she considered her medicine – the bark of the wattle tree. You were supposed to chew it. They'd refused, Rod with some force and derision, and Mary because she wouldn't go against Rod's wishes. Besides, she suspected it tasted terrible.

Janey twisted on her lap, oohing and aahing as she spotted the cat, lethargic in the heat, coming around the corner. Her little blue eyes sparkled. Thank goodness Janey was well and did not seem affected by the hot weather. Now, in the evening it was slightly cooler and this was the best time to work. Mary looked down toward the barn where some murries were fixing the fences in preparation for shearing the sheep. If only it would rain, then perhaps it would really cool off. The sheep could be sheared and then she and Rod could take Janey to Melborne for a holiday. What a wonderful thought! Mary missed her family and her sister, Fiona had been the only one to visit and she had stayed for only three weeks. It had been so nice to have her company.

Sometimes, she thought with a pang, she felt so lonely. Even the scent of honeysuckle made her homesick. Grandmum's house had honeysuckle growing all around it when Mary was a child. So many of her childhood memories were of playing at her grandparents' farm. Her special place to be was sitting on top of the rolling hills where she could watch the sheep. Occasionally, the sheep wandered all the way down the slopes to the beach below where the shipwreck had occurred more than a century ago. When Mary was eighteen years old, she had been devastated by the decision to sell the farm. The land had been in her family for more than one hundred years.

Maybe that was why she was so enthusiastic when Rod suggested they stake a claim and start their own farm on some land he'd heard about in the outback. Mary had moved away with him without reservation. As soon as the house was built, she had planted honeysuckle. At first, everything was wonderful. It was just so hot. There must have been more rain in Victoria she pondered, or maybe the family farm was closer to the city; something was certainly different here. She would never have guessed how isolated she would feel, and how the loneliness would crush in around her.

Mary awoke with a start on the veranda; she felt sick again. Where was Janey? Narana must have taken her. "Narana?"

"Yes, Mum," came the reply.

Weakly, Mary tried to stand up and head for the door, but she immediately collapsed on the floor. Narana was tending her when one of the murries came running up to the house.

"It Mistah Rod! He bad sick down at barn."

Janey started to cry.

Later …

Narana didn't know what to do now. She'd cared for Mary and Rod as best she could. She boiled water and made the healing tea from wattle bark; but it didn't help. It was too late. The bad water and the hot air had been too much for the white family; they weren't as strong as her people. Survival was very hard here. Narana remembered working for white people on a New South Wales sheep station, when she was young and raising her own children. Life there had been difficult for everyone, but it had never been this harsh.

After they had properly buried Mary and Rod, the other murries had left. Narana had insisted on a Christian burial. Maybe the white people didn't understand the earth and how it took care of its own, but they were good people and deserved to be returned to their Creator in the way of their beliefs.

Narana knew about Christianity from what she had been taught at the Mission. Her daughter Daraha was born there and had been baptized by a Christian minister. Narana accepted this as the way of the white people, but she listened to her own messages, the ones she heard from the voices that rode in the wind. Those voices would answer her questions about the baby Janna; she'd just have to listen.

Chapter Two

The Rainforest

6   6   6

As the women walked along the path, they chatted and chewed on white root. Cockatoos screeched overhead waking little Janna up. The women laughed and pointed to the cockatoos and laughed again. Janna opened her big blue eyes and gazed in wonder.

As the sun was setting, Narana tapped Janna on the forehead and said, "You grow up beautiful as sunset" … tap, tap, tap.

Daraha remembered when Narana did that to her, every morning and every night, as the sun rose and set. Daraha was happy to have her mother with her now. They had been apart for a long time, ever since Daraha married Pero, and moved back with him to the rainforest where he worked as a hunter's guide for the white men. Narana did not approve of Pero's work; she had warned him that no good could come of killing animals and birds in the rainforest. Pero said he always made sure the white men only found the weakest of the animals. Besides, he reasoned, if white men liked to hunt in the rainforest, it would keep them from cutting it down here as they had nearly everywhere else. Narana had to agree, because she had worked on sheep stations where all the great trees had been cut down. Narana and Pero both sensed their lack of choice; living in the forest in the way of their ancestors was no longer an option.

Daraha also thought back to when Narana had unexpectedly appeared with Janna a few months ago and asked them to help her raise the white baby. Narana didn't explain who the child was nor why she had brought her into the rainforest. Daraha was surprised that Narana had found them at their camp deep in the rainforest. Normally, she could have tracked them down using the "bush telegraph," a circle of extended relatives who could locate almost anyone, but this time she and Pero had been in camp between hunting seasons and had not been in touch with anyone for several months. Daraha had asked her mother how she had found them. Narana replied that she had listened to the dawn wind each day while holding the red agate arrowhead her father had given her when she was young, and was told where to go next. Daraha wondered if the fact that she was half-caste explained why she didn't follow Narana's ways – listening to messages from the spirits, plants, animals and rocks. Her mother assured Daraha that despite her white blood, her spirit still came from the sky spirits. If she wished, Daraha too could learn to talk to the wind.

Four Years Later ...

Pero watched the boat loom brown and large against the horizon. He waited in the surf, stepping deeper as the boat approached. Pero felt apprehensive. He didn't like this white man. Others he worked for were acceptable, some were even respectful, but this man had a cruel streak. He always took more birds than Pero thought was right. Pero held the boat as the man climbed out. As they dragged the boat to shore, Pero asked the white man where he wanted to go this time.

"Inland, to open country," came the answer.

Pero paused to consider how long the proposed trip would take and guessed why the white man wanted to go there. He shook his head.

"I can't go there, Mistah. Birds nesting, we can't disturb."

The man glared at him and spit out, "I've come all this way to go there and you are going to take me or else...." The man looked at Daraha and her children, who were swimming in the surf nearby. He scowled, "Or else I'll find someone else who will!"

Pero sighed with resignation. He supposed there were one or two others who could do the job, although they were not as skilled as he. Pero had a good sense for the hunt and knew instinctively where to find the birds, just like his grandfather, who had been recognized as the finest tracker around.

Pero and the man loaded up supplies into Pero's boat and set off upstream leaving Daraha and the children behind. Pero didn't feel good about leaving them alone until Narana and Janna joined them in the camp. He knew Daraha always felt more secure when her mother was with her. When they had gone as far upstream as possible, Pero moored the boat and tied it to a tree. He and the man loaded their packs on their backs and started up the trail. As they made their way deep into the rainforest, the sun rose higher and brighter, and soon they were dripping with sweat. Insects swarmed about them producing a persistent drumbeat that reverberated in their ears.

As they walked, Pero reflected back on the past four years. When Narana had suddenly appeared in their camp, he had been surprised and a little irritated, for he knew she wouldn't approve of his tracking for the white man. But the little baby, Janna, had won his heart immediately. She was such a good baby and always laughed when he held her. Besides, Janna had adapted quickly to her new family being close in age to Possum, they were much like twins, both experiencing new things at the same time. Janna also enjoyed having Oonta as a big sister, who was proud to look after them both. Pero had been disappointed when Narana had decided to move to a nearby Aboriginal community, but he understood her need to take care of herself and Janna. It was true he didn't make enough money to support all of them. Pero lived with the fear that the white people would take his children away and put them in a school somewhere far away if he didn't have enough money to send them to a school himself. A cockatoo screech overhead brought Pero's thoughts back to the forest around him. It was the first bird he had heard for awhile, since it was so hot.

Finally, as the day cooled, they reached more open country, a place where Pero knew the birds often nested. Pero loved this part of the country where he had grown up. In the rainforest he often felt smothered, but here in the open spaces he could see for miles out over the rich red soil that formed occasional four-foot tall termite mounds between a scattering of gum trees.

He saw a flash of yellow and whispered, "Ah, there."

They carefully laid down their supplies, and the man retrieved his binoculars. He let out a low whistle as he caught the bird's colours in the sunlight – yellow, turquoise, and red on the belly. There was another flash and a female joined the brightly coloured male. She was yellowish-green with a pale blue underbelly. As they watched, the female flew down from the tree and disappeared in a small hole in a termite mound. Again the man whistled in disbelief.

"I tol' you, they inside termite mounds," Pero whispered.

That night they set up their mist nets and once the campfire was burning and Pero had cooked dinner for the man, he casually waved goodbye and melted into the dark night. He had told the man on their way up to camp that he would be gone overnight, and the man didn't seem to mind. This surprised Pero; usually he had to argue with the white men, who were afraid to be alone in the bush. As he walked away he sang songs and tapped his sticks quietly, telling the spirits that he was coming. When he arrived at the overhang, he lit a campfire and sat staring at the pictures on the walls. He felt welcomed back by the spirits. Reverently, he gently touched the paint on their stone faces, noticing they had begun to fade. This saddened him. He kept vigil with the spirits all night sensing his ancestors looking down on him from the stars. Just before the sun rose, he sighed and bade farewell to the spirits, and walked slowly backwards down the slope, singing the songs of his ancestors.

Pero walked back down the track to where the sky was clearing. The sun had risen and the birds should have been calling, but instead there was an alarming silence. As Pero neared the campsite he knew something was wrong. His heart pounding, he broke into a jog and soon came to the open woodland and the termite mounds. He stopped abruptly and gasped in horror as he saw that several mounds were knocked over. He walked up to one and peered inside; he could see the nest down in the bottom, but no baby birds. He heard a noise above him and saw a flash of colour in the trees. The parrot mother stared down at him as she was joined by the father bird. They weren't chattering in their usual manner. Pero groaned, his heart sinking. He ran frantically to each of the five mounds and discovered that each had the top knocked off and the babies were missing. Then he noticed the white man over by the stream, carefully taking the live birds out of the mist net that they had set the evening before and laying them gently in a large sack. Pero ran over screaming in words the white man couldn't understand

The man bolted upright and backed up against a tree. "Now calm down, Pero! This time you will get part of the profits."

"Profits, I don't want no profits! I tol' you we can't take babies or mums. You promised you wouldn't take." Pero picked up a stick and shook it in the white man's face.

The man laid his hand on the gun in his holster and said evenly, "Pero, put down that stick and calm down. They are only birds. I can get $1,000 for each chick in Bangkok. I'll give you twenty-five percent this time; you will make $6,000."

Pero drew a deep breath, recovering himself as he became aware that the man had a gun. He started to give in to the hopelessness of the situation. Slowly, he dropped the stick and turned away. His head drooped as he began packing up the supplies. The man started down the path back to the boat, carrying the heavy sack of birds. Pero struggled with the two big packs that were left behind. He followed the man back down to the boat, trying not to think about what was happening. It was early and not too hot yet, but Pero was exhausted by the time he dropped the packs in the boat. He watched, feeling empty, as the man gently laid the sack in the bottom of the boat. Pero started the motor and steered down river to the sea.

Meanwhile ...

Janna happily followed her grandmother, Narana, down the trail to the rainforest. They were going to see her family as they did nearly every month. Janna was excited; she loved being in the rainforest and playing with her brother and sister. She wished Narana hadn't decided the two of them should live in town. She missed waking up and hearing the birds singing in the rainforest each morning. But Narana had an important job in the town; she was the town healer. She gathered healing medicines from plants in the rainforest and brought them to the sick. The town people could go to the white doctors, but they preferred Narana. Janna was proud to be Narana's grand-daughter.

The heat of the day was intensifying and Janna could hear the pulsating songs of the insects. She had grown weary of looking for plants. Narana looked back at Janna dragging her feet, and smiled. She knew just what would perk up that little blonde head.

"Come here child, look under leaves." Janna reluctantly walked over and knelt down peering under the bush Narana was holding. A long white root was exposed.

Janna looked up with an excited smile. "You always know where my favorite treat is! Can I dig it?"

"Yes, careful, don't take all, or kill plant, there won't be more treats."

Janna was instantly cheerful; she loved the flavor of the white root. Narana stretched out her hand, Janna took it, and they continued on down the path, Janna chewing on the white root as she went. Narana was naming plants as they walked along, stopping to point out special ones that could be used for food or medicines. After awhile, Janna started to lag behind again, so Narana squatted down and the child climbed on to ride piggyback. As she bobbed along on Narana's back, she played with Narana's hair, twisting it around her fingers. She felt drowsy and finally fell asleep with her hands clasped around Narana's neck.

Narana walked slowly along the bush track. It was getting hotter and she could feel the sweat trickling down her back. She shooed the insects away from her face with her one free hand and carried her knapsack full of special herbs and plants in the other. She felt the weight of the child on her back and smiled with love. What a very special child this is, Narana thought as she reflected on how quickly Janna learned about the plants. Narana knew that her time with Janna would end soon and the child would have to return to the white people's world. She sighed as she remembered how, after Janna's parents died, she'd tried to locate Mary's sister, but the man in the general store at the closest town had refused her entry. So Narana had held the red agate arrowhead that had belonged to her father, and his father before him, in her hand and asked the wind. She followed the advice of the wind and walked to the rainforest, where she knew she would be able to raise the child safely.

It had been a very long, difficult walk, but whenever she was too hot and tired to go on, some shelter appeared. It had seemed the same when she was hungry or thirsty; a plant would be right there to provide her food or drink, and there was always enough water for the baby. Now, four years later, Narana was certain she had done the right thing. They were happy. But yet, in the back of her mind, there was a gnawing and inexplicable fear, which she did her best to cover with love so the fear could never harm them.

Narana decided it was time to rest and bent down gently, lowering the sleeping child to the ground. She reached up and plucked some "warrah" from a tree. She tickled Janna's face with the flowers and laughed as Janna sneezed and opened her eyes. The child pulled the honey-suckle flowers to her nose, and breathed in the sweet fragrance, sighed, and asked for a story. Narana sat on the forest floor, leaned against a tree, and pulled Janna onto her lap. She thought for a moment and then began.

"I'm gonna tell you story 'bout Rainbow Serpent. You know, Rainbow Serpent very special, She made all you see. When the earth was young, everything you see around you now wasn't. No water, no creeks to rest your feet, no trees, no beautiful birds or possums, even no people. Rainbow Serpent came up from bottom of ocean and She entered land just north of here. She made river near where we sleep. She had everything in belly and as She went inland, making creeks and rivers, She let out of tummy all trees and plants and animals and humans. When we see rainbow after rain, we know it put there by Rainbow Serpent to remind us She made everything, and She will always take care of us that why She sends rain. Remember now, we never eat snakes or touch them, because they related to Rainbow Serpent and sacred."

As Narana finished the story little Janna looked up, smiled with satisfaction and promptly dropped back to sleep. Narana felt drowsy too, and closed her eyes.

A while later, Narana awoke and touched Janna. "Wake up, my child or we won't get to camp tonight. Then we won't get to eat."

Janna jumped up and took off running down the path. Narana laughed as she hurried to catch up. The camp wasn't far, she knew, because she could smell the sea. Pero was camping near the mouth of the river these days because it was the easiest place to meet the hunters and transport them back into the rainforest. White men didn't like to walk through the rainforest. Narana caught up with Janna and took her hand and together they walked along the path. Suddenly, a brilliant white, screeching cockatoo flew down right in front of them. The hair on the back of Narana's neck bristled. He's trying to warn us about something, she thought. They followed the path around a large tree and walked right into camp. Oonta and Possum, Janna's sister and brother, came running to greet them.

"Hurry, Hurry!" they shouted. "We go swimming now ya here."

The children were jumping with excitement and Daraha simply hugged her mother, as they all started down the path to the sea. As they walked along, Daraha explained that Pero was out tracking for some white man. She was worried about him because he had seemed unhappy when he left.

The children were playing in the waves and Daraha and Narana were picking up sea crabs for dinner when Narana looked up and saw the approaching boat. Narana stepped backward toward the trees and soon disappeared in the foliage. Daraha stayed and watched Pero navigate his boat out of the mouth of the river and around to the beach. She was glad he was back for she didn't like him being gone too long. Daraha walked out into the surf to catch hold of the boat and steady it so it would not crash on the rocks. Just then, Janna and Possum noticed the boat and started splashing toward it. Janna wondered if the man in the boat with Pero was a white man. He looked very strange. He had a big cabbage palm leaf on his head and his skin was bright pink. Pero jumped out of the boat to help Daraha pull it to the beach. As he did, the boat rocked. Attempting to step out of the boat, the man slipped and reached for Pero for help but fell sideways into waist-high water. He looked so funny when he stood up that Janna laughed out loud. The man looked over at her and gasped. Suddenly Janna had a vision of Narana shaking her head and wailing. This frightened her so that she ran out of the water and up the beach. She heard Daraha call after her, but she kept going. She ran until she was out of breath, then stopped and looked back. The people were only tiny specks on the beach. She strained her eyes and could see them dragging something across the beach.

She walked further around the cliffs and clambered up the sandy trail to the top. At the edge she peered down at the ocean. It rolled and whispered and crashed, sunlight flickering off the waves. A noise behind her made Janna start and almost fall over the edge, but a hand grabbed her arm and dragged her back. At once she was in the warmth, security and earthy smell of Narana's wrinkled brown skin. Nestled into Narana's lap she curled up in a little ball. Narana muttered scolding words, stroked her back and held her tight. Janna curled herself into a tighter ball but Narana rolled her out onto the warm sand. Janna couldn't hold her breath any longer. She splayed her arms and legs out in all directions, giggling and gasping for air. Narana laughed, pulled her to her feet, and they started off, hand in hand, toward camp. As they rounded the large tree, Janna saw the campfire and started to pull loose from Narana's hand. Just then a big white cockatoo screeched from high overhead.

Narana tightened her grip on Janna's hand and pulled her close, saying, "You must always remember your dreaming is arunta, white cockatoo. Whenever you see or hear arunta, it means something very important happening in your life."

Janna's eyes widened at the seriousness in Narana's tone and, nodding her head, she solemnly promised to remember. Janna then turned and ran into the camp.

Later ...

Janna settled down in Narana's lap near the fire. Her mother, Daraha, and her father, Pero, were talking a lot with the strange man. Narana seemed restless, occasionally chipping in with soft words. Narana started to sing softly, and Janna, being soothed soon fell asleep. Later, she woke as her father carried her over and put her to bed with her brother and sister. Possum was whimpering in his sleep and she cuddled down beside him. She lay there quietly listening to the adults talking around the fire. Her father sounded angry, but her mother's voice was soft and pleading. The man's voice rumbled out every so often. Janna couldn't hear Narana and wondered where she was. Janna felt frightened. Suddenly, she felt Narana's body lay down beside her, drawing her close, and whispering in her ear, "Never forget us, my little arunta"

Janna didn't understand and snuggled down into the warm curve made by Narana's body, feeling safe again. She woke up later and looked up at the starry skies. A shooting star made its tracks as the sky was starting to lighten and she felt Narana stir. Her beloved grandmother gently moved away from the peaceful child, got up, and soon disappeared alone down the track.

Suddenly Janna heard a loud crack, louder even than a branch breaking in the wind. Frightened, she had to find Narana. She saw her brother and sister sitting beside the fire, but where were her mother and father? She got up, impatiently brushing the sleep from her eyes, and followed the track that Narana had taken. Her eyes fixed on a ghostly white tree looming beside the track, suddenly, she stumbled over a dark mound. She fell forward across something soft and wet. She recoiled in horror as she realized it was a body. She started to run wildly along the track, crying and calling for Narana. She bumped into something else, it was Daraha, who screamed and pulled her close. Daraha took her hand and started running along the track, dragging Janna behind, until they came out to the headland where they could see Narana's silhouette against the morning sky.

She was moaning and gesturing towards the sky with her hands. As Janna watched, she saw Narana squat down and cover her face with her hands, shaking. She broke loose from her mother's grip, ran over, and put her small hand on the back of her grandmother's neck. Narana took the child in her arms and looked up at Daraha. The sun was rising and the three of them sat close together watching as brilliant colours spread across the horizon. Narana tapped her forehead and said, "You beautiful as sunrise, always and forever, never forget plants in rainforest."

Narana froze suddenly as she looked up and saw the cabbage palm hat man approaching. The two women enclosed Janna in their arms, but it wasn't enough. The man pushed them aside and yanked Janna up by the arm. He waved a gun at Narana and Daraha and shouted, "Stay away! I'm taking her back where she belongs."

Janna screamed and tried to pull away, but the strange man's grip was too tight. Daraha just stood there, motionless. Janna kept screaming for Narana as her grandmother broke through her crying and spoke roughly to the man.

Narana gathered enough strength to approach. She squatted down in front of Janna and took her little hands, "Janna, my little arunta, it time for you to go." Janna wailed and protested not understanding why Narana wanted her to go with this strange man. Narana said, touching little Janna's chest, "You always true Aborigine here, in heart. My little arunta, remember what I taught you. When you look up at stars at night, I will be there watching over you." A cockatoo screeched overhead as Narana kissed her forehead, stood up, and backed away.

Without a word the strange man picked Janna up, threw her over his shoulder like a pack, carried her down to the boat and dropped her inside. Janna screamed which brought Daraha back to consciousness. She walked toward the boat reaching out to comfort her, but the strange man intercepted her, shoved her roughly aside, and pushed the boat off as he jumped inside. He quickly revved the boat motor, and Janna, upset and confused, attempted to scramble over the side to swim to Narana, but the man pinned her down with one hand. The boat sped off, the motor roaring. By the time the strange man let her sit up again, the beach was almost out of sight. Janna flew into a rage, striking at the man with her little fists, but he roughly pushed her away. Caught off balance, she slipped, fell backward, hit her head and blacked out.

Chapter Three

The Suburbs

🌀   🌀   🌀

At Home After School ...

They were whispering again. How Jane hated the secrets shared only by the grownups. When she entered the room, as always the whispering stopped.

"Would you like some tea, my dear?" Mother always served tea when she came home from school if there were visitors. Aunt Fiona was sitting next to her on the couch.

"No." She stared defiantly at the two of them.

"Well suit yourself, Jane. Did you see the pretty flowers Aunt Fiona brought? She knows you love them."

The honeysuckle was in full bloom, its delicate flowers making the air so fragrant. Suddenly Jane wanted to cry. Embarrassed, she ran out of the room.

Later that night, after she'd excused herself from dinner, Jane wondered about the honeysuckle flower and why she always started to cry when she smelled its scent. It seemed to connect to something she couldn't remember, something sad and something beautiful. She pushed herself, but the memory didn't come. When she finally sought sleep, she curled herself up in a little ball.

At School ...

Jane sat staring at the blank sheet of paper on her desk. She had no idea what to write. Her teacher had assigned the class an essay: "Describe your earliest memory of you and your parents. Use at least one hundred words and be descriptive about what you did and how you felt."

It seemed strange, but she realized she couldn't remember anything about her early childhood. There was that time in fifth grade but that wasn't early enough. Her teacher had said early which meant first grade or before. She couldn't remember anything about first grade, let alone anything earlier.

Ahh, yes, she did remember standing in front of her mother and insisting not, under any circumstances, would she be called Mary. She was Jane, just plain Jane. Not Janey, not Mary Jane, but Jane. She remembered stomping her foot and declaring, "My name is Jane!"

Aunt Fiona had stood up for her, taking her side against her mother. It was a good thing too; otherwise, she might have succumbed. She never seemed to get her way when it differed from her mother's. Yes, she could write her essay about this. She must not have been very old then, eight or nine maybe? Maybe older. Was that truly her earliest memory? Were you really supposed to be able to remember such a long time ago? Well, she had better get busy and write. The teacher was giving her a funny look, and her paper was still blank.

Sunday Dinner ...

The next Sunday at dinner, Jane decided to ask her family about her childhood. She hadn't received a very high mark on her essay and she would have to give them an explanation anyway. High marks were a requirement in her family. Plus, it seemed like a good time to ask with Aunt Fiona here for dinner, as she frequently was since her husband died in an accident. There was something about Aunt Fiona's presence that kept her father in a unusually good mood. Under normal circumstances, he strictly forbade her to ask any questions. He was always right; disagreements and even discussions were simply not allowed. That was why Jane stayed in her room and studied most of the time. Her ticket to freedom was to go to University where she could have an opinion and discuss the things that interested her.

Jane cleared her throat, "Papa, I was wondering, could you tell me about when I was a little girl? I can't seem to remember very much."

He looked startled and nearly choked on the spring lamb he had bitten into just before her question. Aunt Fiona patted Charles firmly on the back.

"Oh, Jane, you were always such a good child," her mother said in a disapproving tone of voice.

Her father, having recovered, looked at her squarely, "Jane, you must focus on the present, the past is not important."

Later that night, she could hear her parents whispering again. It was really irritating. Why were there so many secrets? She'd actually summoned the courage to ask them once, but they merely dismissed her saying it was about business. There was nothing to worry about.

Everything seemed fine, Jane thought. They lived in a spacious house. No one ever talked about money problems, not like some of her friends at school. Her family owned Lawton-Starr Corporation, which in turn owned several companies. Her father, Charles Lawton and her Uncle Harold Starr had started the corporation together. Her father still worked there, or at least he went to endless meetings. Uncle Harold, now dead, had been a speculator (according to Aunt Fiona), and had bought land along the coast and started an additional business growing mangoes. Aunt Fiona had built a beach home there, bought scads of new things, and had already taken a trip to America since Uncle Harold died. Jane remembered many important people attending Uncle Harold's funeral. She had seen some of them on the telly.

It didn't make sense; if there weren't any money problems, why did her family need to hide something from her? Jane recalled overhearing them talk about a sheep station, but typically, they always stopped talking when she walked in the room. When she asked about it, she was told that originally their family had raised sheep, and now were talking about their decision to sell the farm. Then they changed the conversation. Maybe the sheep station held the secret. Wasn't thirteen old enough to understand?

◔ ◔ ◔

Sixteenth Birthday Party ...

Why did it always feel like this? Today should be special, her day. But every time she had a party it turned out like this. She was the outsider while everyone else belonged. Here she stood, in the doorway, looking out and feeling alone while the rest of the party was having fun – proof again that she was the outsider. She had asked for a pool party and a pool party it was, of sorts. Her guests were standing around the pool all dressed up, straight out of the pages of a fashion magazine. The pool had an ornate fountain in the middle filled with vibrantly coloured floating flowers. And the music! Jazz tunes spilled from the outdoor speakers. Really, you would think her mother would know kids don't listen to jazz, at least Jane didn't. Jane had actually thought she was going have a party where her friends swam in the pool and listened to their own kind of music and ate pizza. But no! Instead, there were little cucumber sandwiches, radishes cut like delicate roses, and strawberries buried in mountains of cream. The absolute worst part was her dress. It had this ridiculous silk organza overskirt that made her look like an overdressed Barbie doll. Jane was thoroughly miserable. Her sixteenth birthday, God, what a farce!

Jane noticed Doreen, dancing with Warren, giggling as Pam and Peter joined them. They were all having a wonderful time. Aunt Fiona and her father had gathered with the rest of the adults on the other side of the pool. Someone must have told a joke, because everyone was laughing. The guests all seemed happy, except Jane who couldn't help feeling sorry for herself. Why couldn't she be happy?

She spotted her mother coming toward her carrying a big cake lit with candles. The music stopped abruptly while her guests clustered around and started singing "Happy Birthday." Jane tried to duck back inside, but she was too late. Doreen caught her by the arm and pulled her poolside in front of all the guests. There, she dutifully blew out all the candles, while wishing fervently that she would never ever have to do this again.

Camping ...

Jane marched along the forest track, crunching and kicking twigs as she went. She was angry and perhaps a bit sad. She stamped her feet in time to a staccato of words: mad ... sad ... bad ... never ever glad. She could feel the anger boiling up inside her and it suddenly crossed her mind that it might feel good to tear down all the branches and rip them apart.

It had all started when Pam asked her why she knew so much about the bush and the rainforest if she had never been camping before. Jane just knew things about the plants around her. She didn't know why. A lump rose in her throat and tears welled up as she thought about it. She felt angry with Pam for inviting her along. She dragged her left foot, making a deep furrow in the forest floor. A white cockatoo screeched overhead, swooped down and landed on the forest floor in front of her, and an image of an old woman with untidy hair, brown skin and a big grin flashed through her mind. Jane stopped and watched as the white cockatoo strutted on the ground, raising its yellow crest and chattering to itself. It cocked its head and peered at her as it talked away. Suddenly, Jane felt exhausted; she sat down, still watching the bird, and leaned back against a tree root that straggled across the path.

Jane woke with a start and looked around. She must have been asleep for a while as the forest had turned quite dark. She stretched and caught a flash of white out of the corner of her eye; the cockatoo must still be near. Startled, she bolted upright as she remembered her dream.

> *A flock of cockatoos wheeled overhead, screeching at her. One cockatoo came and landed on her shoulder. It started talking to her – or at least Jane seemed to know what it was saying. It told her to find a white root in the forest and chew on it.... Jane nodded, noticing that trees surrounding her appeared luminescent, and were festooned with a sweet-smelling climbing vine – why, it must be honeysuckle....*

The dream faded and that was all she could remember. What a strange dream. Jane realized that the sweet fragrance of honeysuckle was all around her, but she couldn't see it. As always, the scent made her feel oddly melancholy; she thought she might start to cry. But, she was determined to find that white root. She entered the thick foliage, pushing aside the groping branches of forest plants until she reached a small clearing. There was the honeysuckle and next to it a white root poking out of the ground! Tenderly, she broke off a piece, brushed it off carefully, took a small bite and began chewing on it. It tasted like licorice, her favorite candy. Jane started feeling better straight away.

When Jane made her way back to camp, she tried to crawl quietly into her tent, but Pam spotted her and dragged her out by her feet, laughing. "Where on earth have you been? We were worried about you."

"I was fine," Jane said, "Just wanted to be by myself for a while."

That night, Jane tried to read, but she couldn't concentrate so she turned her torch off and lay thinking about nothing and everything. There were so many things she wanted to know. Why were Mum and Aunt Fiona always whispering? Why did her father dismiss the topic when she asked about her childhood? Why did she always feel either angry or sad? Why wasn't she normal and happy like everyone else? Why did the smell of honeysuckle bring up confused emotions? Why, why, why? She went to sleep with questions whizzing around in her mind, her body curled up in a tight ball. Her sleep was restless. At one point, Jane suddenly sat straight up. She heard sniffing around the tent, then some screeching. The next thing she remembered was waking from another strange dream.

A white cockatoo handed her a piece of white root from its beak.

It kept bringing her things: leaves, seeds, bark, twigs, and little insects. Each time it dropped something at her feet it eyed her knowingly, then screeched, raised its crest, and walked away to fetch the next item. The cockatoo brought her so many things in its beak that she lost track of them all.

Then she saw a shimmering pool and a large colourful serpent wriggling beside the water. It slipped into the pool and disappeared. Jane waded into the water which bubbled and hissed. An old woman with brown skin emerged from the water and held open her welcoming arms to Jane. Without hesitation, Jane rushed into the old woman's arms and immediately sensed she was safe and protected.

That was the moment she awoke, feeling safe and warm. She could still feel the rough brown skin of the old woman's cheek against hers. Jane experienced a strange sense of sadness blended with a touch of peacefulness. She took a deep breath.

She decided she better get up and go outside to the loo. Unzipping the tent flap and looking out, she saw something airy floating down in the moonlight. She reached out and caught a small white feather; it looked like it came from a cockatoo. The rest of the night Jane slept deeply. She awakened the next morning filled with a new joy, the feather still clasped in her hand.

Chapter Four

The University

ⓖ ⓖ ⓖ

The Demonstration ...

Jane enthusiastically joined in the yelling and chanting: "Down with Chemicals; Ban 2-4-5-T. 2-4-5-T equals Cancer." She waved her placard with the same intensity and outrage of those around her. When the man in the business suit stepped up to the podium, everyone booed and hissed. The man looked familiar to Jane, and she realized with horror, he's one of the men who plays golf with her father. Confused, Jane lost track of what he was saying as he droned on and on. Someone threw an egg at him and a few people laughed encouragingly. At the end of his presentation, he calmly stepped down from the podium, and as he walked past the students, he recognized Jane and walked over to her. In a loud voice, to be heard over the demonstrators, he inquired, "Aren't you Charles' daughter? Jane, isn't it?"

She shrunk away from him, without answering, as she felt her friends were looking at her curiously. After the man had walked off, her friend Lucy asked her who he was. Jane said she didn't know, but wondered to herself why her father would ever play golf with this man. Although she didn't get along that well with her father, Jane believed that he was an honest and upright citizen. There was no way he would get involved with people from such unethical companies. She thought of all the reported illnesses in the area caused by the use of 2-4-5-T on the sugar fields. One lady was blaming her two miscarriages on the chemical. Jane had heard reports from overseas that supported the woman's claim. "How could these companies get away with what they were doing?" Jane felt her anger flooding back. She held onto Lucy's arm and they went off to find a quiet place to talk.

That night at dinner her father asked about her day at the university. She shrugged and said that all was quiet on the western front which was her usual response when she wanted to close herself off.

But Charles wanted to talk, "Jane," he persisted, as he put down his fork, "I heard some disturbing news. Gary London called and said that you were at a student demonstration today."

"Yes, I was there. I was proud to be there. It is absolutely disgusting what that company gets away with."

Colour flooded her father's face as he rose powerfully from the table and said, "Jane, I want to see you in my study, now." She had never seen her father so furious before. She followed him into the study. She left the door open.

"Shut the door, Jane." And as she softly closed it, he launched in: "Jane, it is about time you grew up. Your mother and I have protected you from a lot, and I can see now it was the wrong thing to do." He took a breath to steady himself. "Jane, the business you were demonstrating against is one of the companies Lawton-Starr used to own. Did you know that? Also, Gary is not only someone I respect professionally, but he is also a personal friend of mine. He and I just played golf together last Sunday."

Although she was intimidated by the intensity in her father's voice and face, she was determined to stand up for herself. "Dad, don't you realize what that company is doing? The chemicals they use are extremely dangerous. One woman has had two miscarriages due to the misuse of sprays, and there are fish dying in the rivers and on the reef because of 2-4-5-T. That company is forcing the farmers to use their destructive chemical or else it won't buy their sugar cane. Dad, I know you don't know about all this stuff. It's important for the public to be informed about this deadly chemical. The company has been covering every-thing up and running false information campaigns." She looked at her father's face and realized that she had gone too far.

Her father's voice was too even, "Jane ... if you ever mention this topic again, you will be out of University and out of home. I will not support anyone who follows such utter rubbish. Your head has been filled with nonsense and if this is the effect that University has on you, I seriously doubt if you should stay on."

Jane knew he was dead serious, but this time she needed to be heard. She stood simmering, wanting to scream every obscenity she could think of at her father. How dare he tell her how she should act or what she should believe! Jane dug her nails so deeply into her thighs in an attempt to temper her counterattack that she could feel the skin breaking. She released the vise-like grip tucking both hands under her. She could feel the sweat breaking out on her chest and under her arms. Her voice shook with emotion, "Dad, this is extremely important to me. You have to believe me. These chemicals are deadly; they cause cancer."

Charles Lawton jumped to a stand so fast she thought for a second he was going to hit her. Jane recoiled and her father appeared startled as though he too was surprised by the intensity of his response. "Jane, this is my final word on this matter. Any further talk on the subject will force your mother and I to take drastic action, do you understand?" He yanked the door open and barreled out of the room before she could say anything. Jane sat there, stunned. She felt numb, nothing, devoid of emotion. All her anger had dissipated and she was left with an enormous hollow ache.

Consequences ...

Jane came down with a cold which turned into a nasty case of the flu. She had a fever, her joints ached and she slept fitfully. When she was awake, she half-heartedly flipped through magazines that her mother brought her. Aunt Fiona came to visit bringing more magazines so that her bedroom began to look like a doctor's waiting room. She could hear her father sometimes, downstairs, but she stayed upstairs whenever he was around. He never came once to check on her. Then the flu turned into bronchitis and Jane coughed her way through many nights. She couldn't find a comfortable resting position because of the ache in her hips. Her emotional state suffered as well, leaving her listless and drained.

Jane spent much of her time while confined to her bed wrestling with decisions concerning her course of study at the University. Plagued with having to choose between her preferred course of study, rainforest botany, or pharmacology. She had managed to keep her options open this long, and she was lucky that the University was willing to let her make her final decisions at this late date. Lucy had already made up her mind to take rainforest botany. Jane wished she had the courage to pursue it as well, but her father had made it quite clear that there weren't any jobs in that field. He assured her he would be able to find her a good job if she graduated with a degree in pharmacology. After the scene in the study, Jane doubted that she could face her father's anger again.

After two weeks she pulled herself out of bed and went to the University, still coughing and blowing her nose. Classes had already begun, by the time Jane resigned herself to gain a late entry into pharmacology. As she came out of the registrar's office she bumped into Lucy, who almost bowled her over with her enthusiasm. They went for their usual coffee together and Lucy, in her eagerness to fill Jane in on all the gossip she'd missed, ended up skipping her next class. Lucy had met some hunky young guy who was crazy about saving the Great Barrier Reef, and they were already planning a trip up north to go diving and fishing. Lucy invited Jane to join them, but Jane just shook her head.

"No way mate, not at the moment. I have too much to catch up on in pharmacology."

Lucy stared at her, "You didn't give way did you? You unbelievable wimp. When are you going to stand up to your father?"

Jane could only smile weakly and shake her head. She could feel the tears smarting at the back of her eyes, but she refused to cry. She heard her sarcastic inner voice say, "Such self-control. You are so brave. You can't even tell your best friend the truth." She excused herself and went to the toilet where she washed her face, took a few deep breaths and returned looking a lot calmer.

"Lucy, I am doing what I want to do, believe me. But listen, I've gotta go. Maybe I'll see you tomorrow."

As Jane sat on the bus heading for home, she felt the tears welling again. She rubbed her eyes vigorously and stared out at the landscape; there was no way she was crying in public. When she was thirteen years old, she had vowed that she would never cry in public again. She never had. Jane sighed as she remembered the scene from years ago quite vividly.

She had been playing happily with some friends at Aunt Fiona's and they had decided to go down the street for ice cream. She was tagging along behind the giggling group when she had caught a whiff of sweetly perfumed flowers. A vision: ... a brown smiling face ... laughing ... gentle hands smoothing her brow ... safety ... happiness ... over-whelming sadness had invaded her consciousness. Her reverie had come to an abrupt end when she realized that everyone had stopped walking and laughing and were staring at her. She was crying and the other kids began teasing, calling her a baby. Jane had turned her tear-stained face away from them and walked back to Aunt Fiona's, where she had sat quietly with the grownups while she wondered why that damn flower always made her cry. She vowed that day that never again would anyone make fun of her for crying.

Sitting on the bus, Jane was still puzzled over her childhood. What was that essay she had to write that time? That's right, "your earliest memory," and the teacher didn't believe that her earliest memory was when she was nine years old. She could still feel the indignation rising, not to be believed really upset her. She guessed that some people are good at remembering things and others are lousy. Look at Gramps; before he died Mum used to say that he would forget what he had done the day before. Jane had the feeling that if only she could remember, she would unravel a puzzle. She laughed at mixing her metaphors: no she meant unravel a mystery or put another piece into the jigsaw.

When the bus pulled up to the next stop, she saw her friend Bob get on and she automatically moved over to let him sit beside her; maybe he would be just the one to cheer her up. She appraised him as he came down the aisle, laughing and talking easily with several of the other passengers. He was certainly good looking and had a lean athletic body. He swung in beside her and tickled her under the ribs.

"Where you been young lady? I thought you'd disappeared off the face of the earth! Anyway, I thought you might need some notes to get caught up in pharmacology, so I was headed over to your place."

Jane looked at Bob with surprise. The last he knew was that she was still deciding between rainforest botany and pharmacology. Jane was annoyed that he automatically assumed she would take the same path as he.

She put on her stupid Valley Girl accent, "Hey Bob, like I've been sick as a dog and looking forward to those wonderful chemistry classes just *soo* much – like especially the chance to see you again."

Bob eyed her sharply, but when she playfully tickled him he laughed it off and relaxed.

University Life ...

Jane stirred, started to stretch out her legs, and ran into something, someone. Bob. He groaned, "It's bad enough you sleep wound up tight like a little ball, but you kick me every morning when you wake up."

"I know, I'm sorry. I wish I didn't sleep like that. I'm always stiff and achy when I wake up." She rolled out of bed, slipped on her robe, and attempted another stretch. "Gosh, do you suppose I have arthritis? I'm too young, aren't I?"

"Not for the rheumatoid kind. It strikes the very young. You'd better go in for tests." Bob had just taken a position as a clinical pharmacist at University Hospital and could be quite irritating when he acted as though he'd just been appointed chief of staff.

As she showered and got ready to go to classes, Jane reflected on her relationship with Bob. She'd met him on her first day of classes at Uni. He was a teaching assistant and doing post-graduate studies in pharmacology. They were immediately drawn to each other, and by the end of her first year, they were spending most of their free time – and most of their nights – together.

Jane felt quite comfortable with him, despite Lucy reminding her that he was a lot like Jane's father. She thought Bob was probably the best part of having to study pharmacology instead of studying rainforest botany. Her choice, of course, had delighted her parents, who had been opposed to her studying anything about the rainforest since she had first mentioned it, after returning from a camping trip when she was sixteen. She had always envisioned doing her post-graduate studies in rainforest botany: she would design a project that used plant derivatives which could be used for medicines.

She knew several important medicines that were made from plants. She felt sure that there were many more which hadn't been identified yet. When she stopped to examine her career fantasies, Jane admitted it was just a way to make herself feel better after being forced to give in to her father's wishes. Her involvement with "Students for Saving the Environment" and her participation in that demonstration were mistakes. She knew she should have realized her family's corporation, Lawton-Starr, was a major player with big companies in the area, and she knew that most of the people her parents socialized with were executives of those big companies. The fact that many of them were on SSE's hit list made her sick to her stomach when she thought about it; so she tried not to think about it.

The best part about her involvement in SSE was Lucy, her best friend. They had met at one of the meetings and they had been inseparable ever since. Thanks to Lucy, she had been able to move out of her parents' house. Her father, over her mother's objections, had even supported her getting an apartment with Lucy. Maybe he had felt guilty for being so hard on her; she never knew because he never spoke of it. Neither had she, for that matter.

Anyway, Jane thought, the apartment was great. There was plenty of room, which they needed since Lucy's Michael, the hunky environmentalist, had been spending so much time with Lucy, and Jane and Bob were practically inseparable. The four of them got along quite well, sharing their ideas in animated discussions over a beer late at night. Lucy and Michael sometimes asked them to SSE rallies, but Jane usually managed to excuse herself without prompting too many questions. Bob, on the other hand, always just laughed and made some joke about pharmacists knowing how to keep out of trouble.

One time though, Jane almost got mixed up in a rally while she was waiting for a bus. One of the demonstrators, a young guy with straggly jeans and radiant blue eyes sat next to her and talked passionately about Australian politics and corporate greed. She was infected by his enthusiasm and attracted to his sparkling eyes. But when he asked her out for a beer, she declined. She got off the bus feeling gloomy and much too conservative. Why couldn't she have gone? Because of her father and Bob, they would both disapprove of her even having a conversation with that type of a guy. Jane sighed, did she really live her life according to them?

She glanced at the clock, "Oh my gosh, I'm late." She had been lost in thoughts. She kissed Bob, threw her knapsack over her shoulder and ran out the door. She arrived at class just in time for the start of the lecture. As the instructor began his lecture, Jane drifted back to her own thoughts again. The talk was boring; so much of studying pharmacology was just memorization. She did like chemistry, though. It was full of possibilities for researching and developing new drugs as well as environmentally safe products. But only the postgraduate students and their supervisors were involved in that. She had been studying pharmacology for over three years now and came through with flying colours, mainly due to Bob's insistence that she pay attention and study.

She was quite happy, really. She and Bob were planning to marry after graduation. Her parents were pleased as they both liked Bob very much. The only problem Jane could foresee were her plans to continue with postgraduate studies. That didn't sit too well with Bob, who had put off changing jobs in order to be with her until she finished at Uni. He wanted to move north where a promising job opportunity with a major retail discount company had presented itself.

Bob had come to the conclusion that being a clinical pharmacist was only a stepping stone to management, where his real talents lay. Not only that, he had insisted that Jane should work as a pharmacist for the same company. Then if he should transfer when he accepted the management position up north, she could transfer and continue working with him at the same company. He was quite excited about his plan, of which Charles Lawton heartily approved. Bob convinced Jane that his promotion to corporate headquarters would take less than three years. At that time she would no longer have to work. She would stay home and have kids. That thought alone, brought Jane back into the lecture hall. She shook her head; she would have to give more thought to Bob's plan.

Graduation ...

Jane sat uncomfortably in the stiff metal folding chair, listening to the speaker drone on and on. Her long black robe and silly hat were hot; sweat was pouring down her back, and her hip hurt. There wasn't even enough room between rows for her to cross her legs which usually helped the pain. She wondered why they couldn't hold graduation ceremonies outside in the gardens. Invariably, the auditoriums were packed and the air conditioning was either too cold, or worse, like today, broken. It was like an oven inside. She imagined her hair was starting to drip. Jane stopped herself, realizing she was being silly. The real problem was that she wasn't happy to be graduating. Now her life would take many dramatic turns, and she wasn't sure she was prepared for them. Every day for the last six months Jane had anticipated this day, when she wouldn't have to sit through those boring pharmacy lectures anymore. Of course, she was grateful to be graduating with honors and to receive a scholarship if she wanted to continue postgraduate studies. She did, and she didn't. She already had accepted Bob's proposal of marriage and was moving up north with him, where she could work as a pharmacist in his new store. Jane looked down at her hand, and admired the brilliant diamond he had given her just last week. She still felt less than enthusiastic about the work part, but she didn't want to disappoint Bob. After all, he had waited for her patiently. On cue, she rose to her feet with the rest of the row and walked up to the podium to receive her diploma. She was graduating. And life would go on.

❀   ❀   ❀

Jane was surrounded by a circle of well-wishers: her family, classmates and friends. Everyone was abuzz about the big party her parents were giving for her that evening. Jane excused herself to go back inside to change her clothes. As she walked toward the building, she noticed a dark-skinned woman talking to Lucy and some of her classmates. They pointed at Jane and as the woman walked toward her, Jane suddenly felt strangely uneasy. A picture flashed in her mind of another dark face with messy hair and a loving smile, an older woman with a white cockatoo perched on her shoulder. Jane shook her head in disbelief as the dark-skinned woman approached holding out an object for Jane to take. Jane gasped for air, everything went black, her knees buckled, and she fainted.

When she came to, Lucy was fussing over her, propping her up and pressing a wet cloth to her forehead. "I guess I just got too hot," Jane mumbled. Lucy helped her friend to her feet, walked with her to the dressing room and stayed with Jane while she changed. She asked Lucy if she knew who that woman was. Lucy shook her head and extended her hand, palm up, containing a red stone, "The woman said something about Narana dying and that the stone was for you." Lucy looked at her friend expectantly.

"Who is Narana?" asked Jane.

"I don't have the faintest, I thought you would know." replied Lucy. "Oh yes," she continued, "She said I was to 'tell Janna not to forget us.' She also seemed really frightened as though she was going to be caught. When you fainted, she looked petrified and clutched her chest. Jane, I didn't know you knew any Aboriginals. She called you Janna. Was she your nanny?"

Jane shook her head. She had no idea. She was even more mystified than Lucy.

Just then, she heard Bob shouting her name from outside the door, and jumped up. "Thanks Lucy. Please don't say anything about this tonight at the party. I'll see you there." On her way out, she slipped the red stone into a hidden compartment of her purse and wondered how she was going to track down the dark-skinned woman who had come to see her. She had to know more.

In the quiet of her room, Jane got ready for the party. She didn't have much time. She had quickly showered, changed and sat down in front of the mirror of her dressing table. She glanced at the long, sleek, black dress she had selected to wear, against her mother's wishes of course. Thankfully, it looked nothing like the Barbie doll outfit she had worn for her sixteenth birthday party. This dress made her look tall and slim, not that she was short, just average. Jane always felt a bit awkward in her body. At least her thick, long blonde hair was an outstanding feature, as were her deep blue eyes. She enjoyed putting on her eye makeup. Her eyes were deep set and angular, very much like her Aunt Fiona's. Strange, she mused, I don't look at all like my mother. Jane stood up, straightened her dress, looked in the mirror and approved of what she saw. "Not too bad," she was pleased.

The party was a grand affair, as were all of her mother's parties. There were luscious strawberries and rich cream, along with lots of little cakes and the champagne flowed like water. All of her father's business associates were present as usual, each one saying all the right things.

When the party had reached a festive high, Charles Lawton asked the crowd for silence, raised his glass, toasted his daughter, and handed her the keys to a brand new Land Rover. It came as a total surprise to Jane. Before she could recover, her father, his glass raised high again, announced the engagement of his daughter Jane to young Bob. With obvious signs of pleasure on his face and great ceremony, Charles welcomed him into the family.

Jane was aghast. She hadn't even thought of making an announcement. Once again, her father had taken over for her. Suddenly well-wishers rushed in on the young couple. The men, joking and laughing, kept pounding Bob on his back, extending their good wishes, and talking excitedly about his new position. Jane was somewhat pushed into the background, occasionally receiving a peck on the cheek from a well-meaning family member or friend.

Later that night, after the guests had finally left, Jane excused herself. She was completely exhausted. She kissed Bob good night and approached her father.

"Really Dad, I love the Land Rover, and the party was very nice, but I had no idea you planned to announce our engagement." Jane must have sounded a little tense, because her father dismissed her remark with a gesture as though shooing away a pesky gnat, replying sharply:

"Nonsense, my dear. It was the perfect opportunity. All the right people were here." He bent down slightly to receive his daughter's kiss on his cheek.

Helen, Jane's mother, chimed in with words in support of her husband, "Darling, it would have been at least a month before we could have had a formal engagement party for you; and your father is so proud of Bob."

Jane forced a weak smile and said, "It's okay. Please forgive me. I'm just extremely tired. It's been a big day. The party was marvelous, Mother. Thank you for everything. Good night, all." Walking up the stairs she heard Bob and her father start talking business. Jane just sighed. "Men!"

In the quiet of her room, she slipped out of her party gown and suddenly remembered the strange red stone. She took it from its hiding place in her purse, and examined it for a long time. The stone was shaped like an arrowhead. She wondered about the woman who had brought her the stone, was puzzled about the name Narana, and wished desperately to know the connection. She was too tired to think about it any longer, and slipped the stone under her pillow. Maybe she'd have an answer in the morning. Jane curled up in a ball and quickly drifted off to sleep. Pictures began to form in the still of her mind and dreams came to tell her a story.

> *She's looking everywhere, in the bushes ... around all the trees ... the birds screech; where is it ... why can't she find it? She is on the beach, searching, she is under water, where is she, why can't she find her? She panics ... she is drowning ... reaching ... screaming....*

Jane awoke. She was all tied up in her tangled sheets. Even her head was covered. What had she been doing? She could only remember looking for someone or something, and then nearly drowning. She got out of bed, walked to the window and stretched. Her hip ached. There was a flash of white in the trees. Jane sighed deeply, climbed back into bed and fell soundly asleep.

Chapter Five

Wedding Plans

⑥   ⑥   ⑥

Jane sat on the veranda, looking through the wedding magazines and trying to be excited. The luncheon would be served in a little while; even appointments with wedding consultants and Aunt Fiona were being turned into formal affairs. She sighed. It had only been a few weeks since graduation, but it seemed like forever. So much had happened. Lucy's wedding was fabulous. It was so simple. She and Michael had planned the entire affair themselves and were so relaxed. How Lucy had managed that was totally beyond Jane's comprehension. Jane wished she could have an outdoor wedding, too. Just the thought of getting married standing under a tree, made Jane feel peaceful and content, like everything was right with the world. But everything wasn't right.

When Lucy was planning her wedding, Jane had asked Bob about doing something similar but a little more formal. Bob had joked that they could get married on the golf course, which was sort of his idea of the great outback. Her parents had both registered their objections immediately. Helen definitely wanted a large formal wedding and her father insisted that she be married in the church. So she was stuck. Besides, she figured, if she fought to get her way, it would probably end up raining or being unbearably hot.

Everyone was excited about the coming event, everyone except Jane. All the fuss, planning, and parties made her a nervous wreck. Her hips hurt more than ever, especially her left one, and some mornings she thought she should go to the doctor. She wondered if it was her old bed causing the pain. She had moved back home after Lucy left, because her father had refused to continue paying for the apartment. Her mother had been sure she wouldn't be safe alone, and even Bob had supported her parents' views. Having accepted the new job, Bob had already moved north to Wainton to be close to the new store he was opening. The plan was for Jane to live at home until the wedding and help her mother with all the arrangements. After the wedding, there would be a brief honeymoon, and they would go up north together where she would take a job in Bob's new store. The bright side of moving there was that it was very close to where Lucy and Michael had settled. The down side was that she probably never would get to do her post-graduate studies. This made her feel like a failure.

Her mother walked out onto the veranda, "Have you found some pictures you like dear?"

"No, Mum, not really. Oh, they are all nice, it's just that none of them seem to be me."

"Well I'm sure the consultant will have lots of marvelous ideas. She is regarded as the best in the city. She planned Doreen's wedding, you remember Doreen Cox, don't you? Her father is CEO of that mining company."

Jane nodded; she didn't want to think about that company, with its asbestos mines. What a terrible mess. All those poor people; and her mother wanted her to have a wedding like Doreen's. Crap! Is there no justice? Jane wondered.

Her mother had prattled on with hardly a pause, "Pink, pink, all those lovely shades of pink. Even the chandeliers were covered with pink ribbons."

"Mother, please, I don't want pink anything, not even underwear!"

"Jane, don't be crass. You can have whatever colours and flowers you want as long as it looks beautiful."

Jane heard the door open, and Aunt Fiona appeared. Thank goodness, Jane thought. Maybe now we will have some sanity. Ms. Wyatt, the wedding consultant arrived moments later – sanity was short lived. As Jane was being introduced to Ms. Wyatt, a flock of kookaburras in a nearby tree started laughing raucously. Jane smiled, the birds knew exactly what was going on here; in fact, all this hoopla was "for the birds."

By the time lunch was over, Jane had looked at hundreds of photos. She had resigned herself to doing whatever made her mother happy, so there would be much less hassle. They had made all the necessary appointments to meet with the caterer, the dressmaker, the hatmaker, and the florist. They were now discussing the colours for the bridesmaids' dresses.

"Actually, my favorite colour is purple," Jane said sharply. She was getting tired. Her mother wrinkled her nose.

Ms. Wyatt looked at Fiona and quietly suggested, "Perhaps it would be best if we picked the flowers first; then it would be easier to decide on the wedding colours."

"Oh yes, it is the wrong season, you may not be able to find your favorite flowers." Fiona commented.

"Thankfully!" her mother sniffed. "We certainly don't need Jane sobbing all the way down the aisle because it's lined with honeysuckle."

Jane glared at her mother, stood up, and marched into the house. She heard her aunt say, "I guess we shouldn't have brought that up." Jane didn't wait to hear more. She grabbed her purse, ran out the front door, hopped in the Land Rover and soon she was heading down the street toward the freeway.

About sixty kilometers out of town, Jane pulled off the main highway onto a bitumen road, which led to the state park where she remembered camping when she was a teenager. It was a beautiful park which had once been a farm and now was being returned to its natural state. She parked, got out and climbed the hill slowly, favoring her left hip. She gazed with delight at the green grass and the gum trees that stood on neighboring hillsides. Jane started feeling better as soon as she left the city. Now, except for being irritated with her mother and having a dull ache in her hip, she felt terrific. She inhaled deeply, taking in the freshness of the air. As she started down the path to the gully, she recalled the last time she had been here. She had been angry then, too. Jane didn't remember why; it was something Pam had said. Yes, it was Pam. They had been friends since secondary school, and Pam was going to be one of her bridesmaids. But Pam wouldn't have been any help with today's crises, as she herself had always made fun of Jane's weeping over the honeysuckle. It was so frustrating that it happened every time, and no one was the slightest bit sympathetic. If she only knew why honeysuckle made her cry, then maybe she could get past it. Maybe she would try hypnosis. Fat chance Dad would pay for that! He thought all psychological therapies were utter nonsense. Even if they were, though Jane disagreed, there had to be some explanation why the scent of honeysuckle made her cry, and she wanted to know what it was.

Jane ventured deeper into the forest down a steep path. After just a few steps she found herself in another world. She forgot all about her problems as she observed the fern trees looming tall overhead. It was unbelievably dark in here without a glimmer of blue sky in sight. There were many different varieties of ferns growing, more than she could identify. The path continued straight down and was beginning to get slippery from all the moisture.

Suddenly Jane saw a huge tree; its trunk was bigger than any tree she had ever seen. She started to walk around it and discovered by peering into a large hole that the whole tree was hollow, yet it was still alive. She looked up. Yes, there were leaves and apparently some new growth. As she continued circling the tree, counting her steps as she went, she noticed that an orchid had attached itself to the tree and was in full bloom. She smiled. That is it; the flowers for her wedding, Orchids! It was comforting to be here and find such a simple solution to what had been a very frustrating question. The tree seemed to beckon her, and when she had finally finished her tour around the outside, she stepped inside and looked up. It was entirely hollow and big enough for a family to camp inside.

Once again, an image of an old woman with untidy hair, brown skin and a big grin flashed across her mind. Jane suddenly felt safe and loved. What a strange sensation, as though the air around her was electrified. She shivered as goosebumps rose on her skin. Jane sighed. It was so good to be here. Suddenly she remembered the woman at her graduation, the one who had given her the red agate arrowhead. Could that woman be connected to this place? Why did she seem so familiar? Now Jane was in a state again. Why did she have all these thoughts? What was going on? She stepped out of the tree, and looked back inside. What just happened?

She hiked up the hill. The birds were singing as though everything was right with the world. As she emerged from the forest onto the hillside a group of cockatoos flew to a tree on top of the hill. When she got back to the Land Rover, Jane dug through her purse until she found the arrowhead. She held it in her hand for a few moments and then laid it in her lap as she drove off.

When she arrived home, her father was just getting out of his car. "Hi Dad," Jane greeted him, as she opened the door and slid down from the high seat of the Land Rover. The arrowhead bounced down on the driveway. Her father leaned over and picked it up for her. He looked at it and then at Jane, raising one eyebrow, "Where did you get this?" he demanded as he handed it back to Jane.

Jane's face flushed as she said falteringly, "I … ah … a woman gave it to me after my graduation ceremony. She was waiting outside for me. I didn't know her though. I think … uh … Dad did I," she hesitated, "have an Aboriginal nanny?"

Her father's eyes narrowed as he listened to her. He caught his breath. "No!" he said sharply, "you definitely did not. The woman probably mistook you for someone else."

"I don't think so, Dad. Lucy said…."

"I don't care what Lucy said," her father scoffed, cutting cut her off mid-sentence. "The woman made a mistake." He turned and walked to the house. "Come on, we're late for tea."

Jane followed him, but she was annoyed. He always treated her as though she were still a child. Thoughtfully, she laid the arrowhead on her bedside stand and went to wash up for tea.

While they ate, Jane's mother, kept up a running commentary on the planning session they'd had that day. Her father scarcely spoke, and her mother was delighted when Jane announced she wanted orchids for her wedding.

When Jane retired to her room later that evening, she thought about just how pleased her mother was about the wedding plans, and she decided to be more cooperative. But, as she sat down on her bed, she noticed the red arrowhead and was reminded of the conversation with her father. She took the arrowhead in her hands, and as she did, she felt electricity all around her just like when she was in the big tree. This was just too weird. Maybe her father didn't know anything about the woman, but someone must. As Jane curled up in bed, she decided she would ask Lucy help her solve the mystery.

She smells the smoke of a campfire and hears voices. There are so many birds singing. She sees the flash of a brightly coloured lorikeet in the treetops. A white cockatoo settles on the bush next to her. Kookaburras laugh hauntingly from a tree overhead.

As she rounds a large white tree the birds' voices grow noisier, arguing.

Suddenly, a loud crack startles her. Jane is running and running down the beach. With every step her feet sink deeper in the sand. The water rises, covering her head. She struggles to find safety, gasping for air....

Jane awoke drenched in sweat, disoriented. She reached for the lamp and knocked something off her nightstand. Finally, she found the light switch and looked to see what had fallen. It was the red agate arrowhead. As she reached down to pick it up the dull ache in her hip intensified. Turning back over, she stretched out allowing her hip joint to relax. She tried to remember her dream, but it was all jumbled and quickly evaporating from her mind. She just remembered being frightened, and that there was a forest and a beach. She had similar dreams a lot lately, but she always woke up before she ... before she drowned! Jane shook her head to clear her mind, took a deep breath and reached for the aspirin bottle and her glass of water. Perhaps pills would help her hip and then, maybe, she could sleep peacefully.

The Bridal Fitting ...

"At last, a chair!" thought Jane as she sat down in the shade of the umbrella. She had spent the last three hours shopping with her mother; she was tired and the pain in her hip was unbearable. She wasn't used to standing for such a long time.

"We've managed to accomplish a few things this afternoon, but there is still so much to do. Have you decided on the bridesmaids' gifts yet, Jane?"

"Well," Jane paused, "I like the opal necklaces."

"Yes, they are nice. But do you think they will go well with the dresses since they have high necklines? Have you thought about bracelets instead? Anyway, we had better order our drinks if we are going to get to the fitting in time. Waitress!" Helen raised her hand to catch the woman's eye.

Jane ordered a lemonade and sighed pleadingly, "Mother, I'm not sure I can stand for a long time at the fitting; my hip really hurts."

"Oh, does it really hurt that bad? I'm sorry!" Her mother reached over and patted her hand. "It won't take very long, dear; you'll be fine."

Jane looked up gratefully at the waitress when she brought the lemonades. She took two aspirin from her purse and swallowed them with her first sip. She hoped the pills would help. She was actually looking forward to the fitting because Lucy would be there. She had come home for the weekend a bit early to try on her matron-of-honor dress. It seemed funny to think of Lucy as a "matron," but her mother had insisted that this was the correct title. It would be even more amusing when her mother figured out that Lucy was pregnant and the straight, long-sheath style dress her mother had insisted on probably wouldn't fit Lucy by the important date. The wedding was still more than a month away. Her mother and Lucy would both come apart at the seams. Jane smiled at her pun.

"That's better," Helen said, noticing Jane's smile. "I told you a rest and a drink would help." She knew her mother was trying to be nice. Helen loved all this planning and shopping and organizing, while Jane would much rather be reading or camping, or doing anything else. It seemed there was constant underlying friction between them; maybe all weddings caused this tension. Jane didn't know, but she would be relieved when it was all over.

"Finish your lemonade, Jane. Don't you want to stop and look at the paper napkins one more time to make sure the colours match the ribbon before we go to the fitting?"

"Mother, I'm sure they match. Besides, I'm not sure I can walk that far and we only have fifteen minutes to get to the fitting."

"Of course you can. Don't you think you can keep up with me? After all, I'm twenty years older than you."

Jane's mother was asking rhetorical questions again. She had always done that as long as Jane could remember. The questions weren't really questions at all. It was as though they were designed to lead Jane to what her opinion should be or remind her that her opinion did not count. It was so annoying.

Her mother stood up. "Are you ready, my dear?" Jane got out of her chair slowly and stretched her hip. It still hurt. She couldn't remember it ever being this bad except early in the morning, and that pain always went away with the warm shower. She clenched her teeth and hobbled along after her mother.

When they arrived at the dressmaker, late of course, Lucy and Pam were already there. Doreen had showed up too, even though she wasn't in the wedding. All three were laughing so hard they were nearly doubled over. When they noticed Jane and her mother arriving, they straightened up. It was quite apparent why they were laughing. Lucy was already showing and looked ridiculous in the tight fitting dress that wouldn't zip up on the side. Jane heard her mother gasp.

"Hello Jane, Helen." Doreen greeted them enthusiastically. "I hope you don't mind my traipsing along with Pam today. I just love planning weddings. In fact, I'm thinking of starting my own business as a wedding consultant. Speaking of consulting, I think you are going to need a consultant to figure out how to get Lucy's new body into this dress!"

Everyone, except Helen, began laughing again as Lucy did a pirouette in front of the mirror. Helen went over and sat down in the only chair available to collect herself. Jane decided she didn't want to be present for the impending tirade, and asked the clerk if she could be shown to the dressing room to try on her dress. When she returned, Lucy was wearing a different dress, in a similar colour, that fit better but wasn't nearly as spectacular as the original one. Helen's face was taut. Doreen and Pam were chattering away and Lucy looked irritated.

"I'm sure we can find a dress that will work," Jane attempted to console her mother. The situation didn't seem as funny as she had anticipated. "Do you like my dress?" Jane twirled around in a cloud of white when a severe pain shot through her hip, which simply gave out. She collapsed in a heap on the floor.

The Diagnosis ...

Jane was disgusted with herself, lying here in this hospital bed, not allowed to get up. The doctors were scheduling all sorts of tests and had given her pain medication, which made her so groggy that she hadn't even been able to talk sensibly to Bob on the phone. She was more clear-headed now as she wondered how long she had been in the hospital; and where was everyone? Probably taking care of her mother. The shock of it all had nearly given Helen heart failure. Jane remembered the look on her mother's face when she realized that Jane really could not get up.

Just then Aunt Fiona stuck her head in the door. "Hello, my dear. You poor thing! To think you have been in all this pain and no one has paid a bit of attention to you. You need lessons on how to complain! You could just follow your mother's example." Fiona smiled to show she was joking.

"How is Mother?" Jane asked.

"She'll live, that is, if she doesn't have to postpone the wedding. She is already wringing her hands and moaning about not being able to get another church date for at least two months. Your mother has an amazing sense of priorities." She paused becoming concerned. "How are you really, my dear?"

Jane looked at her aunt and replied honestly, "I don't know. The pain is dull now. I think I'm okay, but it would be nice to know what happened. I'm a little frightened."

As they were talking, the doctor walked in. He greeted them both and started to examine Jane. In answer to Jane's questions he responded, "We won't know for sure what it is for a day or two. There are several tests we need to do to rule out some of the more serious diagnoses, but with your history it is most likely an exacerbation of rheumatoid arthritis."

"My history?" Jane queried. "You mean the pain I have had in the early mornings? Is that typical of rheumatoid arthritis? What causes it?"

"Well, the cause is unknown. However, it is thought that the immune system is activated in such a way that it actually attacks the synovial membrane of the joints. An episode could be caused by physical or emotional trauma, shock, fatigue, or even a severe infection. Certainly, any of these could trigger an exacerbation of the disease. However, I am referring to the severe strep infection, extremely high fever and prolonged illness you had when you were a child."

Jane was confused. She didn't remember a fever or any joint pain until she was at Uni. She looked at her aunt with questioning eyes.

Fiona excused herself, saying she would see if Charles and Helen would like to come in to talk with the doctor.

Terribly upset, Jane bombarded her parents with enough questions that her parents and Aunt Fiona explained that she had been extremely ill when she was young. They thought she had rheumatic fever and kept her in bed for several months. She finally recovered, without a heart murmur, which had ruled out rheumatic fever. She had also suffered from joint pain, which the doctors called suppurative arthritis, a childhood disease characterized by inflammation of the joints, that is frequently caused by a strep infection. Helen and Charles said they wanted her to have a happy childhood and put it all past her and had agreed never to discuss it in front of Jane.

Jane was furious, but before she could say anything, Bob walked in, obviously worried. He had flown down in a company plane and come directly to the hospital. After all his questions had been answered, Jan and Bob were left alone in her room. Worn out, Jane fell asleep holding Bob's hand.

A Change in Plans ...

When Jane came home from the hospital a few days later, a family meeting was held. Aunt Fiona was there along with Bob and Lucy, who had stayed in town because she was so concerned about Jane. After a lively discussion, for Jane's family anyway, everyone decided it was best to postpone the wedding indefinitely. Jane was obviously not well enough to see it through at this time. Helen, of course, was utterly disappointed and quite upset about the prospect of having to cancel all the arrangements. At least the invitations had not been mailed yet. Helen said she would send handwritten notes to close friends and associates explaining the cancellation so everyone would understand. Jane would go ahead and move north to live with Bob for now, and they would get married later. Jane thought her mother would have a stroke when Bob said "live together." Strangely enough, her father had agreed – and so it was settled. Jane was relieved. She had thought she would be pressured to go on with the wedding even if she were in a wheelchair, and she didn't want that. Jane had come to the conclusion that, deep down, she wasn't ready for marriage, although she didn't share this with anyone except Lucy who promised not to breathe a word. Jane also sensed Aunt Fiona under-stood and was supportive, even though they never discussed the subject.

Shortly after the family meeting, Bob caught a plane because he needed to get back to work. Jane, Lucy and Aunt Fiona decided to drive up to Fiona's beach house, where she and Lucy would stay for a couple of days before continuing the trip north. When they set out on the road, Jane finally began to feel relieved.

Jane sat watching the landscape, mile after mile. Lucy had been driving the Land Rover for quite a while now and probably would need to stop soon and turn the wheel over to Fiona. Jane couldn't drive yet since she was still on crutches. The pain in her hip was ever present, except when she took her meds. The doctors assured her that, although her condition was chronic, the pain would not always be this severe and that she would soon be able to walk without crutches. In fact, the doctors even wanted her to exercise.

Jane was lucky the arthritis was not present in other joints, just her hips. Usually it spread to all the joints in the extremities. She had asked why the pain had intensified so dramatically now, and one doctor suggested that the stress of the upcoming wedding could have been a factor. That had seemed to satisfy everyone, but Jane knew it went deeper than that. She hadn't told anyone except Lucy about the nightmares. She'd assumed her father's refusal to further discuss the woman and the arrowhead meant that she would get no information from anyone else either. That was the way it had always been in the past. Her father laid down the law and it was not questioned or even discussed again. In fact, when she thought about it, Jane realized that even the reason she'd chosen pharmacology was *not* to go against her father's wishes. The SSE demonstration was the closest she'd ever come to rebelling. Somehow, she didn't feel safe unless he approved of her choices in life. She wondered if her relationship with her father was the reason she kept dreaming about drowning. Probably. She was grateful her father hadn't been upset about putting off the wedding. He really liked Bob for which pleased her.

Bob was so supportive. He'd been there for her all the way though her studies at Uni, and now, even though he was so busy with his new store, he had taken time off to be with her when she was so sick. She felt lucky to be with such a caring man. She did want to marry him, but something about the wedding had felt wrong. She guessed it was the stress of all the planning, the many parties and all the rest. Did everyone else enjoy them? The social activities her mother enjoyed had always made her unbearably nervous, including her sixteenth birthday party. Oh yuk! She didn't want to think about that.

Jane turned to Lucy sitting beside her in the front seat and said, "Aren't you getting tired? We should stop soon."

"Sure," Lucy replied. "I imagine you would like to get out and stretch. How's the hip holding up?"

"Not too bad right now. Aunt Fiona, are you asleep back there?"

"No, just lost in thought. Actually I was thinking that I should introduce you to my massage therapist. He does wonderful massages and acupressure. Maybe he could help relieve your pain."

"Maybe," Jane sounded doubtful. As a pharmacy student she had been taught to be wary of alternative therapies. On the other hand, she was also aware and concerned about the side effects of the drugs she was taking.

"Do you get massages regularly?" she asked her aunt.

"Yes, I do and I find it to be quite invigorating. Many of the aches and pains which I developed over the years have disappeared since I started regular massage sessions. Truthfully, though, I have learned some other techniques that have helped substantially, too. Learning to breathe correctly is probably the most important. And I've learned to use acupressure on myself when I feel out of sorts.

"Me too," chimed in Lucy. "I use acupressure on a specific place on my wrists when I have morning sickness, and it really does help the nausea go away quickly."

"Okay, I'm convinced" Jane conceded, "why don't we all go for a massage."

"You know, he'll probably come out to the house since there are three of us. He has a portable massage table." Fiona sounded excited. Jane moaned to herself. What was she getting into? What does one wear for a massage? Before she could ask, Lucy had flipped on the turn signal and was heading for a rest stop.

The Decision ...

The entire stay at Aunt Fiona's was wonderful. Jane felt completely renewed. The massage had been great, and as Wong, the therapist, had suggested, focused breathing did seem to help her control the intensity of her pain. She decided to practice the breathing technique every morning before getting up. She also relished spending so much time with Lucy and Aunt Fiona, and being able to hear the sound of waves anytime, day or night. There were wonderful birds, too; lots of lorikeets and cockatoos in the trees around her aunt's house. She could easily live in a place like this. But then, she always had an affinity for a more natural environment. It was so much nicer than in the city

She tried to imagine the place where Bob lived. It sounded like it was right in town. Maybe she would be able to persuade him to move. Admittedly, she was a bit apprehensive about moving in with him and working in the pharmacy department of his store, although no one expected her to work until her hip was much better. She mentioned her concerns to Lucy as they left the beach house and drove north. Lucy suggested she might want to work for Michael instead; Lucy thought there was more desk work than she could handle by herself, especially since she had been gone so long. Also, when Jane felt like it, she could do some environmental field work, which, although it was very hot most days, was outside near the beach or in the rainforest, where Jane liked to be. Anyway, Michael was going to have to hire someone to replace her, since she would be staying home with the baby for a while at least.

Not only that, Lucy was excited about the idea of having Jane work with her. Jane, too, was enthused by the prospect. She had never been too enthusiastic about being a pharmacist in the first place, and she was finally admitting the reality of that to herself. The only obstacles were Bob, and, of course, her father, but if her hip hurt too much to stand behind the counter all day and count pills, what could they say? She would see.

Chapter Six

Up North

ⓖ　　ⓖ　　ⓖ

The CD ...

Jane sat on the patio of the Tree House Cafe which faced the main shopping street in Wainton, waiting for Lucy. They were to have lunch together, but Lucy must be running late. Music from a store on the other side of the street drifted across to hcr. Thc words of the song came through during a lull in the conversation around her:

> *"If the company won't take care of me…*
> *If the company won't treat me right…*
> *Who's gonna feed my babies,*
> *Who's gonna treat them right."*

The lyric triggered thoughts about the company that bought all the sugar cane from the local farmers. The company had a large factory south of Wainton. Sometimes, the wind blew from the south and the stench from the factory could be overwhelming. Jane had also heard rumblings that they didn't treat their workers very well.

Lucy turned up at that moment and Jane stood up and gave her a big hug. It was so rare that they had any time to be alone together to talk; she considered these times precious. Lucy had the baby to care for, plus working with Michael, but she occasionally managed to slip away to spend an hour or two with Jane. Jane was grateful that Lucy's mother, Marilyn, who had sold her home in the city and moved to Wainton when Lucy was at Uni, was happy to babysit on these rare occasions. It was much easier to talk without little Mikey crawling around your feet, spitting food onto the floor, wailing, and generally being adorable but demanding. Lucy apologized for being late. They were burning off sugar cane fields along the road to town which aggravated her asthma, slowing her down. Besides, it always upset her as it did Michael, that the rainforest was being torn down to make way for sugar cane fields.

Lucy's big news was that she and Michael were having another baby. She was so excited, and wanted Jane to be the first to know for several reasons. First, because they were best friends and secondly, because she would not be coming back to work after the baby was born, which meant there would be more office work for Jane. She could work full time if she wanted. Jane tried to explain to Lucy she wasn't sure she would be able to keep working for Michael after the wedding, but before she could, Lucy had finished her lunch and dashed off. Jane had a second cup of coffee by herself, thinking about what to do.

To her surprise, she heard the same song as before from the music store across the way and, after paying her bill, she wandered over to the store, and asked the young clerk behind the counter what music was playing. He handed her the CD cover; although it wasn't her style of music, she bought it anyway because the words had intrigued her.

At home that night she played the new CD and listened to the words of the first song very carefully. The words were angry and bold, ranting about the destruction brought on by governments and big companies. The music made her feel restless and agitated. While preparing dinner, she slammed the cutlery around. That always made her feel better. Throwing cutlery into the sink, how stupid was that? Jane wondered. Bob was coming home for dinner soon, so she told herself she better get organized, shower, and clean up the kitchen. What would he think of her if he saw her like this? She turned the music up loud and jumped into the shower. She was still enjoying the music while she was drying off when she heard the music suddenly stop. Irritated that he would just turn off the music, she called out in a disgusted tone, "I suppose that is you, Bob."

Bob appeared at the bathroom door. "What is this trash you're playing, girl? You know that band has nearly started riots. I wouldn't play their music in this town unless you want to be lynched."

"Oh come on Bob, I think you're a bit off here. This is a free country. We do not live in the Deep South of the United States, and we are not blacks. Anyway, it's only music." Jane replied tensely.

Bob glowered at her, "You fool, don't you know they are singing about the Big Reef Refinery this whole town works for, to which all the farmers around here sell their sugar cane? Without that company we would be nowhere; our retail sales would plummet, and we would probably be out of business."

Bob was yelling. He left the bathroom and stormed through the kitchen. Jane attempted to quell her anger and started getting dressed thinking that Bob was probably worried about the upcoming merger of his company and Blue Star, a large discount chain owned by Lawton-Starr. He had been working on the merger for months and was quite tense most of the time. Jane could hear him prowling in the living room, muttering to himself and probably cleaning up. He always liked things perfectly arranged and often spent hours tidying things up when he got home.

She brushed her hair back, applied some pink lipstick and slipped into a pretty dress. She looked at herself in the mirror and was worried about what she saw: she looked haggard and ugly. There were bags under her eyes. She hoped she would sleep better tonight. Her hip had acted up again last night, and although she took aspirin and used her breathing technique, it seemed to throb and kept her awake.

Dinner did not go very well. Bob remained in a rotten mood and took it out on her. Finally, he said he needed to go back to the office and told her not to wait up. After he left she noticed that he had taken her new CD. "Bastard," she muttered under her breath. Jane started to feel herself slipping over the edge again. Many unsettling thoughts were running through her head as she made a cup of tea and got ready for bed. Bob was always angry with her unless she played the perfect fiancee. All he wanted was her to be there for him, wear pretty dresses, and socialize with business colleagues and their wives. He didn't like her working for Michael, in fact, they usually argued at least once a week about her work. It was not that she especially enjoyed office work. It was just there. And, it got her out of the house and her mind onto other things. She liked working with Lucy and Michael, even if they were all so busy they seldom had time to talk. She did love the fieldwork, however, she was doing less of it as time went on. She used to go out in the field at least once a week, but she hadn't been out in a month now.

Michael had expanded, hiring more technicians, and since Jane only worked three days a week, he tended to give her more of the office work. Besides she and Lucy split the office time, so they were only together one day. When Lucy left to care for the new baby, Jane would lose the opportunity to do field work. That reminded her, that she was going to get to go out in the field tomorrow. The technician was sick so Jane had been assigned to take water samples at the estuary where the river met the sea. That would be a welcome break.

Her thoughts turned to the upcoming wedding. There seemed to be so much to do, and Jane still couldn't summon any enthusiasm. Her mother was in charge of all the planning this time around; no one wanted a repeat of the last fiasco. Jane was going to arrive home only at the last minute to play her role. Her father seemed excited about walking her down the aisle. She thought of her father and how he always remained so closed. He said he loved her, but she often felt the emptiness of his words. His love was conditional and only evident when she lived by his standards. He had not approved when she decided to work for Michael, instead of working as a pharmacist in Bob's store. It had been unusual for her to defy her father's wishes, but with Lucy's support, she had managed to stick to her guns.

She wondered about her parents relationship; Helen did everything Charles said. Sometimes Jane wondered if her mother might be afraid of her father. Why don't some women ever stand up to the men in their lives? Jane acknowledged that it was a failing of hers as well. She let out a nervous giggle, thinking of Bob's distorted face when he spoke in outrage about the controversial CD. Oh well, she comforted herself, tomorrow is another day. She snuggled into a tighter ball.

When Bob came to bed, his movements woke her. Her hips were aching again. She uncurled and straightened out. She took a sip of water from the glass by her bed and slipped an aspirin down with it. Maybe she should ask Bob to bring home something stronger, aspirin never seemed to dull the pain enough at night. She hadn't had a good night's sleep for over two months now. She wondered how much longer she could go on, but she didn't want to take steroids and that was probably the next step. Bob sleepily threw his arm over her and drew her close. Finally, the warmth of his body soothed her hips and she fell into a restless sleep.

> *A man is chasing her ... a loud noise, a shot ... there is blood ... then moaning and cries..... A cockatoo flies up and drops a snake into her lap....*

Jane opened her eyes and realized it was morning.

The Gun Shots ...

The sea gulls were making a nuisance of themselves. They were always hungry. Jane wondered why she wanted to be here, testing the water for sediments. It was hard work and almost unbearably hot. How she longed to jump out of the boat and into the water, but she knew it wasn't safe. There was so much sediment; the poisons were condensed here at the mouth of the river. Recently there had been a noticeable increase in the number of dead fish floating in the river. How would the gulls survive? The shoreline should not have been compromised, Jane thought angrily. The rainforest had ensured the purity of the water for centuries, but now that it was nearly gone, there was no protection. Michael believed this destruction was also doing severe damage to the Great Barrier Reef. He had been diving offshore from this area a few months before and discovered some disturbing changes. Consequently, the Department of Natural Resources had given him a grant to test the sediments from the river to see if it was the same as that found on the reef.

Jane started the motor and moved the boat up river to do some sampling. Suddenly, shots rang out. She threw herself flat in the bottom of the boat. Where were the shots coming from? The shore? Another boat? She had to get out of here! Jane put her hat on an oar and raised it level with the side of the boat. No shots. She raised it a little higher. Nothing. She sprang to the helm, started the engine and took off out to sea. She looked around; there were no boats in sight. She felt sure the shots had come from shore. She turned and headed north, up the coast. After several minutes she stopped the boat and let it drift. She tried to stop shaking. Why had she been shot at?

Back at the office, she had filed an incident report and told Michael what happened. At first, Michael acted as if he didn't believe her, until he went back to the dock with her and saw the holes in the side of the boat. He was puzzled. Who would do such a thing and why? Michael tried to dismiss it. Perhaps it was only kids playing with guns, or hunters. Jane disagreed. No, it was a warning. She could feel it. There was something very wrong here.

⑥ ⑥ ⑥

That night Jane dreamt of the shots....

> *She is running along the beach ... someone yells ... more shots.... She runs faster and faster, until she falls ... exhausted.... She looks back and can barely see someone dragging something across the sand.*

Jane awakened, trembling, wrapped up tight like a ball. The dream seemed so real. She lay quietly, not wanting to disturb Bob. She hadn't told him about the shots and hoped Michael wouldn't. It would only give Bob more ammunition as to why she should stop working for Michael and come to work for him. Besides, Michael had promised to investigate the incident, and she wouldn't go back there, so she wasn't in danger herself. The dream continued to disturb her and she couldn't shake the feeling that it had actually happened. As Jane started to go back to sleep, she remembered having similar dreams when she was living at home and planning the wedding the first time. In these dreams she was always running down a beach and then almost drowning. Maybe that was why this dream was so real, because she had dreamt it before. She breathed a sigh of relief and moved her hip into a more comfortable position.

The next morning, Lucy called. Michael had told her about the incident and had spoken to one of his buddies at the state Department of Natural Resources. Michael learned from his friend that there was a ring of poachers working that area and that the DNR had been trying to catch them for some time. An officer would like to talk to Jane if she were willing;

he would stop by at the office at eleven. Jane agreed and then hung up. She hoped she didn't have to file an official report, because she really didn't want Bob to find out. She hurriedly straightened the bedroom and bath and got dressed. A button was missing from her skirt and when she opened her sewing basket to find a needle, she saw it – the red agate arrowhead.

Suddenly, the memory of all the dreams came flooding back to her, only they seemed more like visions than dreams. She sat down stunned, feeling light-headed. She remembered the woman who gave her the arrowhead. Somehow she felt there was a connection.

When Jane arrived at the office, Lucy was there. The officer was talking to Michael. Jane was introduced and she told him exactly what had happened. Jane didn't think her input would be very useful, but the officer assured her it was. He told them they were planning to send an under-cover agent back to repeat the work Jane was doing the day before, in hopes something would happen a second time. Lucy and Michael were obviously excited by all the drama. Nevertheless, Lucy noticed that Jane seemed somewhat detached. When she asked why, Jane simply handed her the arrowhead.

"I think there is a connection." Jane said simply.

Lucy looked shocked. "What do you mean, a connection?" she pushed.

"All my dreams are the same, and more than that, it feels like I've been there before."

"Been where before? I'm really confused. Let's go for lunch and talk. Mother has Mikey; I'm sure she won't mind if I don't make it home for lunch."

Before they had even ordered, Jane related every detail of her dreams that she could remember. Actually, some things seemed clearer now than they had in the past.

Jane explained that she believed there was a connection between the arrowhead and the nightmares. The content of her dreams was remarkably constant since she'd moved up north. They were not really nightmares, as she remembered them, until night before last when she had the fight with Bob. Then, the incident at the river occurred. It was a bit eerie that she happened to find the arrowhead this morning, which she didn't remember seeing at all since she moved.

Lucy listened intently. "I agree Jane, I think that the circumstances seem to be more than a coincidence. The truth is, I have thought all along that you should find that woman and talk to her. There are just too many things in your life that seem a little strange to me, like your crying when you smell honeysuckle, and that woman just appearing at graduation. She definitely knew you."

"I know," Jane answered ruefully, "I've always been afraid to ask questions, but something in the back of my mind makes me aware that my life is a puzzle with a piece missing."

"Well, let's not worry about it right now," Lucy patted her arm reassuringly. "I'll do some checking around to see if I can learn something about that woman, and maybe get some answers. Now, let's order, I'm starving."

Remembering ...

A few days later Jane found herself standing in front of a cement house in an Aboriginal town just a few miles from Wainton. Jane introduced herself when the dark-skinned lady answered the door.

The woman didn't look surprised, "Hello! I'm Daraha and I knew you when you were little girl, and I knew one day you'd come see me."

She brought Jane inside and offered her tea. Jane declined and sat down on the worn sofa. She tried to explain that she didn't remember anything about her, but Daraha raised her hand as if to silence her and started in on a long story about how her mother, Narana, appeared one day in the rainforest holding a little blonde haired, blue-eyed baby. She continued for some time and Jane just sat staring at her, not believing she could possibly be the child in this woman's story.

"So Janna, sorry, uh' Jane, your mother and father died on sheep farm and Narana took you and looked after you and walked all the way to rainforest to find us. You lived with us for over four years. You know, Narana loved you so much. She tried teach you everything she knew. She healer, you know, she knew every plant that made medicine in the rainforest.

"You know, when that poacher man came and took you away, he killed my Pero, my husband. I thought I'd die from grief. I was lucky, I had Narana with me. She looked after children and me for long time. Then they came and ask many questions and took Narana away. You know, they try an charge her for stealing you. Unbelievable." Daraha shook her head at the memory. "Narana never recover from that, you know. They pretty rough on her in courtroom. She stood up there, proud as anything, she not gonna give in, but they broke her in the end. They called her bad names." Daraha broke into tears at the memory.

Jane sat motionless looking at Daraha. She didn't believe a thing she said. There was no way. Suddenly she felt sick. "I have to go now," Jane stood up and started for the door. Daraha held out her arms to embrace her, but Jane panicked and felt as though she was going to throw up right in the middle of the floor. "Let me go! I don't believe you.

I don't believe any of this." Jane pushed past Daraha and ran out the door.

Once in her car and on the road, Jane regained her composure. She had managed not to throw up and was feeling more in control. Then she realized that she had been driving for some time and hadn't reached the turn for town. She looked around and didn't recognize where she was, nor could she figure out which direction she was going. She was becoming more and more confused. Suddenly she noticed a road to the right that looked vaguely familiar, so she turned. She traveled a short distance when the road abruptly ended. By the time she had come to a halt the wheels of her Land Rover were sinking in the sand. Thankful she had four wheel drive, Jane jumped out to lock the wheels in so she could shift down. As she did so, a white cockatoo flew down, almost landing on her head. Startled, Jane jumped. She calmed down as the cockatoo landed right in front of her and started walking away. It stopped and looked back at her, called out as though it were beckoning to her, and started to walk away again.

Jane was mesmerized. The scene resembled those of her dreams. That bird wants me to follow it, she mused, astonished. Strange idea? Why not?

She reached in the Land Rover to get her key, saw the red agate arrowhead on the seat and picked it up. She turned to follow the cockatoo, which stood watching her with unblinking little eyes.

Jane followed the cockatoo, and realized the sandy road they were on was turning into a forest track. She couldn't tell which direction she was walking in, but she thought the ocean couldn't be too far away. She kept following the bird as it flew ahead a little way, dropped to the ground and waited for her. Flashes of sounds and

confused images spun around in her head. What was going
on? As she came upon an old white tree, she felt a tearing
pain in her gut and doubled over. She saw visions of *a body
in front of her ... brown skin ... everything went dark ...
hard to see ... red on her hands ... she heard screaming.*
Suddenly she realized that she was the one screaming.

She vomited, then weakly drew herself to her feet and
looked around, dazed. She walked along the track to the
headland, too confused to know exactly where she was
going. She concentrated on breathing as she walked. She
was breathing as deeply and slowly as she could; she could
feel her heart pounding. She started to shake and wail as
more images came. *It was her Aboriginal father lying dead
on the ground. She saw a man with a gun.* Anguish and
despair overwhelmed her. *A big black hole loomed in front
of her, as she started to slip into it, falling into the nothing-
ness.* She screamed again, lost in the terror of the moment.
As her hand clenched tightly in an effort to hang on, she felt
the arrowhead bite into her hand. She looked up in pain and
saw the evening star blinking at her. Her heart expanded as
a voice said, *"If you can see the stars, I am there with you."*
She let the sobs rack her body. *The black hole turned into a
starry night sky.* She lay there, too exhausted to move.
Much later she came to her senses, shivering. It was
twilight. Gradually, she sat up and brushed the sand off her
face. She struggled to stand, and then slowly searched for
the way back to her car.

It wasn't far, and when Jane tried to back out, the
Land Rover pulled easily out of the sand. She felt much
better now, clearer. She made the conscious decision not to
think about what had happened. She just wanted to find her
way home so she could collapse. She was glad she would be
alone; she had waited until Bob was in the city for a meeting

to go to see Daraha. Jane didn't have the energy to share her experience with anyone. When she got home, she took the phone off the hook, ignoring the blinking answering machine and went directly to bed.

The Next Day ...

Jane sat on the sand dune, staring mindlessly at the waves. She hadn't really believed Daraha when she told her that she had lived in the rainforest and about Pero's death. It all seemed to be too much. Her first reaction was, "No way, I know that didn't happen because I would have remembered something that important." But now, the story explained the experience she had yesterday. She had actually remembered finding the body. The experience seemed so real, emotionally and physically, even spiritually maybe, if that was a way to really know something. She still hadn't recovered from the incident. Her body felt drained, and her hip hurt so much that just walking along the beach was a struggle. So she chose to sit and think. She reflected on the fact that the pain had increased dramatically since she graduated from Uni. That coincided with the time she had first seen Daraha, when she had given her the red agate arrowhead and disappeared. All the dreams started after that point and her hip problems had increased drastically.

The doctors, who had diagnosed the pain in her hips as rheumatoid arthritis, had told her that although chronic and painful, it didn't have to be debilitating. Jane reviewed all the explanations. It could be caused by physical or mental trauma, shock, fatigue or even severe infections. This news alone had upset Jane, but it was too much for her to take when her family admitted she had been sick as a child and bedridden. Learning this about her past had been quite enlightening. Jane accepted this explanation as the reason there always seemed to be so many secrets in her house when she was growing up. She had rationalized that her childhood illness must have erased her early childhood memories. But now ... even if that were part of the truth, there was apparently a whole lot more. No wonder she had been so sick. She felt numb. Numb was okay, good even. She didn't want to experience any more emotion. It was just too much.

The Reaction ...

Still in pain, Jane hobbled around in a daze for the next couple of weeks. She told Lucy of her strange experience in the rainforest. Lucy believed the whole story, dreams and all. Michael was more reserved in his response, and suggested she should confront her parents for the truth about her childhood, or at least talk to Aunt Fiona

Contrary to her friends' response, Bob was furious. He didn't believe a word of it and demanded to know where to find the black bitch who had told Jane these lies. Jane was confused. She had believed in Bob but when he expressed such disgust and fury, it negated all her own feelings. He acted as though he knew everything under the sun, and worse than that, he knew what was good for her. Shouldn't she have a right to make up her own mind about what to do? Even if only parts were true, the mystery about her childhood remained. Jane had to know the truth.

Bob kept up his tirade for days until Jane was worn to a frazzle. Finally, when she felt she could take no more, she lost control. She literally pushed Bob out of the house. When he tried to come back in, she created quite a scene, screaming and running through the house, destroying everything she could lay her hands on that was Bob's or anything he had even given her. She was like a mad woman. She smashed his tennis racquet, threw everything associated with him, including her diamond, out the front door and into the street. The neighbors were peering out their windows, but she didn't care. Bob was aghast. She had hardly ever argued with him in all the years they had been together. When she wouldn't allow him back into the house, he gathered up all that was left lying in the street and left.

An hour later Jane's phone rang. It was Lucy. She asked if she could come over for a talk. Bob had called her and Lucy wanted to know what was going on. She was worried. When she arrived she found Jane cleaning up some of the mess she had created and attempting to calm down. Lucy told her that she had spoken to Jane's parents who were all upset after speaking with Bob, and wanted to come and see her. Jane had no intentions of seeing them now or ever. Finally Lucy convinced a very confused Jane to at least talk to Fiona.

Chapter Seven

The Truth

🌀   🌀   🌀

The stripe down the middle of the highway had a hypnotic effect on Jane as she drove. It was nearly dusk and she still had a long way to go before she'd reach Fiona's beach home. When she thought about the events of the past two weeks, she still broke out in a cold sweat. Her whole world was a lie. Was there even a smidgen of truth in anything she had been told? Jane didn't know what to believe. All these years she had been living someone else's life. She had been controlled on all fronts, never being allowed to be herself. The only thing she knew for sure was that she felt an immense relief, as though she had just finished performing a very demanding role in a long-running play. Now she planned on sleeping late, going for long walks and gradually rediscovering herself. Maybe, just maybe, she could figure out who the real Jane is. That's the gift, just as Lucy said, "You will find a gift in all this Jane, look for it." She could finally see what the gift might be now, if only she could be strong enough to face herself.

Her new knowledge did little to dull the anger she felt towards her parents and Fiona. How could they not have told her who she was? Did they think they had the right to play God? It was her life, after all, not theirs. Aunt Fiona was going to have some explaining to do; and this time, no lies! Jane remembered when she was in the hospital and diagnosed with rheumatoid arthritis, that part of her decision to postpone the wedding was because Aunt Fiona – no, Fiona, there was no reason to call her Aunt Fiona anymore, she obviously wasn't her real aunt – had suggested that sometimes illnesses were signals from our bodies telling us that the choices we had made were too stressful and perhaps not our best choices. Fiona had brought this up when they were discussing her childhood illness and her parents' decision not to tell her about it. However, somewhere in the back of Jane's mind, the suggestion had made her wonder if perhaps Fiona thought that the wedding was not a good choice. Part of her ultimate decision to postpone the wedding was her belief that all the planning was just too stressful; the other part of her decision was a sense that perhaps she should stay independent for a while.

Nonetheless, she had stayed with Bob, moving up north just like they were married. She had let him run her life too. Wait, hold that thought, let him run her life. She realized she could have made a different decision. She could have pursued post-graduate studies, as she had originally intended. Instead she had gone to work for Michael, conducting environmental studies in the rainforest. It had seemed the best way to get back at her father. She had won by refusing to be a pharmacist, hadn't she? She had spent the last two years with Bob yelling at her all the time, getting shot at while she was taking water samples, having frequent nightmares, and nearly deciding to take narcotics to control the pain in her hip. Was she acting out some sort of suicide wish to get back at her parents? But this was before she knew about the lies, wasn't it? Jane felt bewildered. She saw the beginning of the mango groves which meant she was near to Fiona's place. Soon she would have some answers. At least she would know who she was.

At Fiona's ...

Fiona sighed. She had always known that Jane would be angry when she found out about her past, but she had never imagined that the truth would be this devastating for the young woman. Of course, if it had been up to Fiona, Jane would have been told the truth when she was young. Charles had made them swear never to speak of it. Helen had readily acquiesced. Harold, Fiona's husband, had been so prejudiced against the Aboriginal people, he had actually pressured the authorities to try the poor woman who had cared for Jane for kidnapping.

From the start, Fiona had felt uneasy about Harold's fury and revenge tactics; after all the child had been well taken care of and Narana was such a gentle soul. The memory of Narana saving Mary's life after Jane was born convinced Fiona that Narana had meant no wrong by taking the child to the rainforest. But there was little Fiona could do to stop Harold. In the end, desperate to help, Fiona had hired a lawyer for Narana with her own money and not told Harold. It came to light in court that the man who brought Jane to Harold had been a poacher, and that Harold had paid him a huge bounty for finding Jane. The poacher admitted to shooting and killing Pero, Narana's son-in-law, in order to take the child. This turned the court's sympathies toward Narana. It was difficult to believe the poacher's claim that Pero had threatened his life and he had shot him in self-defense. The version of the story told by Daraha, Pero's wife, and by Narana rang of the naiveté and sadness that truth in such situations often has. Ultimately, Narana was found not guilty. Fiona knew she had done right by defying her husband, although she decided to keep her investment secret.

Fiona revealed all this to Jane piece by piece, and tried to calm her down.

But Jane just kept walking in circles, wringing her hands and mumbling over and over, "That woman loved me, I know it, I have felt her presence with me several times and now she's dead and I can't even thank her for caring for me."

Fiona felt terrible about this. Daraha had come to see Fiona one time when Jane was a young teenager, begging Fiona to bring Jane to see Narana one time before she died. Evidently Narana was so broken by the rigorous trial that she never recovered. Daraha hoped at least to give her mother the final gift of seeing Jane before she departed. When she learned how Fiona had gone to Helen to request the forbidden, Jane went over the top, screaming in agony and disbelief.

"How could you? And my mother, she is not even my real mother. Who is my mother? And how did you get me? I hate you all! All those secrets, the whispering. I remember it so well. I asked about it and was told it was about business. And then you had the gall to tell me I couldn't remember anything because I was sick. What did you do, drug me?" Jane began sobbing uncontrollably.

Fiona escaped to the kitchen to make more chamomile tea, hoping it would help Jane calm down. When she returned to the sitting room with the tea, Jane was gone. Fiona felt a wave of fear, but then she noticed a breeze; Jane must have left the air-conditioned house in favor on the humid night air of the veranda. As Fiona approached her, Jane said dully, "Please continue the story. First I would like to hear about my real mother. How did she get on that sheep farm?"

Fiona explained that Mary, Jane's mother, was actually her and Charles' younger sister. Mary had been enamored with Rod's desire to sheep farm because she had fond memories of spending so much time as a child alone with her grandmother on the family farm in Victoria. Mary had been very upset when Grandmum died and the family opted to sell the farm.

Fiona mentioned the shipwreck as well as the history of the farm and family. She added that the blanket chest that Charles kept in the guest room had survived the shipwreck. As Fiona talked, a wave of calm washed over Jane. She could envision the chest and how she liked to take the old clothes out of it to play dress up. She had not realized the clothes were that old, although her mother, Helen, scolded her once telling her that the clothes were not to be played with as they had belonged to her ancestors. Although she had not totally understood what ancestors were, Jane had decided that some day the chest would be hers. Now, that she knew that it was so important to her real mother, she felt adamant it should be hers. In fact, she would take it when she went to the house to get the rest of her things.

Jane could not bear the thought of ever living with Charles and Helen again. She told Fiona so, and Fiona attempted to defend her family's actions, but to no avail.

Jane maintained her anger saying, "I still can not understand why everything was kept so secret? Who decided never to tell me and why?"

Fiona thought for a minute and then suggested that Jane attempt to look at the situation from the family's point of view, "Just to try to see our side," she encouraged her. Jane scowled, but nodded her head. Fiona began.

"I think it is important for you to know some of the family dynamics so if you will bear with me I will tell you our story from my point of view." Jane nodded, curious partly because this was the first time anyone in her family had actually talked to her like she was an adult.

"I think the situation may have been partially created because I was the oldest, and very aggressive for a girl. I did everything first; I was even the first woman in our family to go to University. I was quite rebellious and tried every way possible to defy my father, your grandfather. He insisted that I become a teacher. Since I didn't want to do that, I took business courses instead, thinking I could get a job with some big company when I graduated. I certainly did not want to live on a sheep farm and teach at the local girls' college. Besides, I wouldn't inherit the family farm; Charles would, as he was the only son. This irritated me a lot! Men inherited businesses and women got married. The upshot of all my rebellion was that I did end up getting married to a young salesman who worked for the same company where I had taken a job as a secretary after graduation. Harold was good looking and a smooth talker. He had big plans of becoming a millionaire by the time he was thirty-five, and I believed everything he said. Charles thought Harold was the best, and they became fast friends.

By the time Charles had graduated from Uni, he no longer wanted to farm. The land was worth a fair amount of money and Father, who had worked hard all his life, wanted to retire and live near a golf course. So after Grandmum died, the family decided to sell both houses and the whole farm. Mum and Dad retired, Harold and Charles invested the rest of the money in their new business, a sugar cane refinery up north that Harold knew was on the market and would make a fortune if managed correctly. Mary was much younger and she was quite upset at the thought of giving up the farm. She had spent several years living with Grandmum after Grandfather died and was much more attached to country life than Charles or I. Even though she was just a teenager, it was no surprise when she up and married Rod Rivers. He was an adventuresome young man who loved the land. His parents were dead and he lived with his grandparents who didn't own any land. His only hope was to go to the outback and start his own farm."

Jane interrupted. "I still don't see how you created the situation. It sounds like my mother made her own choice."

"Well, yes, but she was so homesick. I only went to visit her once and she didn't ever get her share of the money. All the money went into the business and she was promised her part with interest later. She didn't...." Fiona's voice faded. "I'm sorry, Charles and I loved her very much. We felt extremely guilty when we learned of their deaths. I blamed Harold, which is probably why he was so angry with Narana. I wanted to raise you instead of Charles, but he pulled rank on me."

"Rank? What do you mean by that?" Jane asked curiously.

Fiona thought for a while and then said, "You know how rebellious I said I was? Well, not really. The men made all the decisions. Occasionally I would offer an opinion, but I usually found an unobtrusive way to say it. When Harold made a statement, it was the final word. Oh, I could tease him and get my way sometimes. He was really nice to me, always quite charming. Actually I seldom questioned his decisions. I think if I had stood up to him, or Charles, maybe some things would have been different for you."

"Well I can sort of understand as I have been that way myself, but what about Mo – Helen?" Jane caught herself just in time. "Why couldn't she have told me?"

"Jane, you know how very formal your mother, sorry, Helen is. She never breaks a social rule; and the first rule is never disagree with your husband, at least not in public. Also she is terribly concerned with social status. She came from a rather well-to-do family, who regarded Charles and Harold as young upstarts, even though our family had been landowners for more than a century. Helen has always tried to live up to her mother's self-proclaimed social status. The scandal that surrounded your return to our family and the trial was a bit too much for Helen's family. That's basically why you have never been to your grandmother's home. They speak, but the relationship is strained. So you see, Helen didn't want you to know either. She wasn't being mean. She just lives in her own world and didn't see the point of ever discussing anything about your past. Every time I brought it up, she would get frightfully upset, and insist that I whisper."

"Oh, that accounts for all the whispering I heard, but everyone must have known, I mean with the trial and all?" Jane looked more curious than distressed.

"You're right," continued Fiona, "but the scandal died down quickly, mainly because Harold paid off all the newspaper publishers he knew, which was probably all of them. Even then, Harold and Charles were rather well-known businessmen and everyone who knew them knew about Mary's daughter being found in the rainforest. Actually, the talk may have dropped off more because you became so sick than for any other reason."

Jane raised her eyebrows. Fiona replied, "Yes, you really were very sick, for a very long time. We didn't lie about that. Actually no one lied at all. We just didn't tell you anything. I would have told you more, especially after you postponed your wedding, but you never asked. You simply went on with your life and I thought perhaps it best if I didn't stir things up."

"Oh, Fiona, if you only knew. My life has been hell." Jane started to sniffle, but then took a deep breath, and continued, "I really want to know more. Tell me about the family businesses. Truthfully, I never paid any attention. Then with all the press about the maltreatment of factory workers and the environment, I thought that my family must be involved in all the dirty business tricks there are. I would ask Charles, but you know how he treats my questions."

"Actually Jane, I've never taken much of an interest in the business either. I should, considering I own forty percent of Lawton-Starr. Charles sits as chairman of the board in my place and votes my shares and his twenty percent and Mary's twenty percent. Well, I guess that twenty percent is actually yours, but I seem to remember that we put it in a trust for you, and Charles is the trustee. The first company Charles and Harold bought was that sugar refinery that is just south of Wainton. We sold it for a huge profit. Actually they invested in several companies, but Charles was reluctant to invest in some of the businesses that Harold did, so Harold owned several separately. He was quite the speculator. He usually made decisions on the spot when given the opportunity to invest in anyone or in any company. He was so flamboyant with his decisions that he was frequently in the news. His notoriety presented him with many opportunities to invest. Lawton-Starr Corporation now owns several of those companies.

"After Harold died, we sold a few of his businesses and decided to expand others. A couple of the companies weren't too stable and, for a while, there was a recession and we needed the cash, so Charles thought it best to sell stock in the corporation to raise money. Most of this happened when you were too young to pay any notice. Oh, and Harold did achieve his goal, he was a millionaire by the time he was thirty-five. Actually, I believe he would have gone into politics if his parachute had opened and he had made a soft landing instead of crashing into the desert the way he did." Fiona stopped and took a deep breath.

Jane eyed her aunt, "I'm sorry. I shouldn't have asked."

"Oh no, it is all right. I'm quite happy now, and in some ways very happy that things worked out the way they did. Not that I'm happy Harold died, mind you, but I've learned a lot about myself that I don't think I would have learned if I had continued living in Harold's shadow. Lately, I have been considering taking a more active role in the corporation. I, like you, am disturbed by some of the business activities that I read about. Since I'm benefiting from those decisions, I think it is irresponsible of me not to know what is actually going on. In many ways, the experience you're going through is reopening my eyes to a lot of things I haven't thought about in a long time. For one thing, I need to see Daraha and tell her I'm sorry for not doing more than I did during the trial. She'll probably kick me out, but I shall try anyway".

"Aunt Fiona," Jane's voice had lost its harshness, "perhaps we could go together. I wasn't very nice to her when I went there. I was so shocked at what she told me, I screamed at her and ran out the door. It is time I apologized."

There were tears in Fiona's eyes as she stood up and held out her arms to Jane who embraced her, weeping softly.

The Next Morning ...

Jane's attempt to sit up in bed was stifled by a shooting pain in her hip. Her leg wouldn't move. The thoughts in her head began a downward spiral. This was all their fault. So many terrible things had happened to her it was no wonder she was sick. The doctors had told her this could happen again. The severe mental trauma she had suffered could cause an exacerbation of the arthritis, and it had. She couldn't even get up to go to the toilet. She reached for her aspirin and water and screamed out in anguish as the pain shot through her left hip. Fiona came running into the room to find Jane crying uncontrollably. "They'll have to give me steroids this time. Just look what you all have done to me," she screamed at Fiona. "I can't even get out of bed."

Startled, Fiona stepped back and surveyed the situation, attempting to stay centered as Wong had taught her. She took a slow, deep breath, consciously thinking about her energy field and keeping her boundaries intact. She walked over to Jane and laid her hand on her head.

"Please try to calm yourself, Jane. Take some deep, slow breaths. That's it," she said as Jane started to comply. "When you feel in control, I'll help you sit up. We will take everything slowly. That's it." Fiona kept encouraging Jane. "Remember the breathing technique Wong taught you. Let's practice that together." As Fiona gently led her through the breathing exercise, her voice had a calming effect on Jane and she started to relax.

After about ten minutes, Jane looked up at Fiona, smiled weakly and said, "Thank you." Fiona put her arm around Jane and helped her to sit up in bed. When Jane winced, Fiona reminded her to keep breathing. Jane swallowed the aspirin and water Fiona offered her and then asked hopefully, "Do you think Wong would come see me?"

"I think he might. He doesn't normally make house calls anymore, but I still see him regularly in class, I believe he would come this once," Fiona replied.

"In class? What sort of class? Are you learning acupressure?"

"Well. not exactly. Our class is studying energy." Fiona smiled when Jane looked puzzled. "Each of us has an energy field around us and our life energy runs through our bodies. It's fascinating to learn about because whatever is happening in our energy field determines how we feel, both mentally and physically."

Jane looked lost. Fiona said, "I'll tell you what, let's call Wong and see if he can come over. Then he can explain this concept more fully." Jane nodded and Fiona went to make the call.

When Wong arrived that afternoon, Jane was sitting in a chaise lounge on the veranda watching the waves and listening to the birds. "Ah, a very healing environment, Miss Jane. Would you like for me to set the massage table up out here. It appears to be very private."

"Oh yes, that would be perfect. Did Aunt Fiona tell you what has happened to me?"

"She mentioned you had suffered trauma and I can see your energy field is weak and dark." Wong squinted as he peered at her.

Jane prompted him, "You know, Wong, I'm interested

in learning more about energy. Aunt Fiona told me a little about it this morning after she helped me use the breathing technique you taught me when I was here two years ago. It really helped me relax. But I've never found it to be effective when I use it by myself."

"That's because she sent you energy to help you while she talked about breathing. Then, when your energy field increased, you felt better."

"Really? I don't understand how this energy works, but I do know I was absolutely a mess this morning. I thought I would never be able to get out of bed again, but with Aunt Fiona's help, I bathed and managed to walk out here. My hip still hurts a lot, but I was be able to breathe through the pain and take one step at a time."

"That is good," Wong said. "Now we will stop talking and begin the treatment. I will help you onto the massage table."

Wong worked on Jane for a long time, sometimes touching her body, sometimes holding his hands above her. He occasionally reminded her to breathe deeply. She drifted off and saw beautiful colours in her mind, all the colours of the rainbow appeared one by one, then the colours came together and shimmered like a long snake, then melted and turned into a beautiful white light. Jane was not conscious of any pain. She was surprised when she heard Wong's voice.

"You may lie here for a few moments if you wish, and then I will help you move back to the chair. Your energy field looks much better now. I shall go in and find Fiona. Please wait for me to assist you in getting up."

Jane took a long breath and listened to the lapping of the waves. She heard a cockatoo screech. She smiled and thought, "those cockatoos are always around me." She

laughed aloud when she saw the white flash of a cockatoo
flying above her, jumping from one tree to the next.

That Week ...

Jane saw Wong every day for the next few days. Her
hip pain had diminished considerably although it had not
gone entirely. But, then again, it really had never entirely
ceased since she had been in the hospital. Now she could
walk without a cane and could regulate her breathing effectively enough, she didn't need her aunt to assist her in the
mornings. She had drilled Wong with multiple questions
about energy and, although she didn't fully comprehend the
concept, she understood that energy came from the life
force within her. Wong explained that when she practiced
the breathing technique, what she was really doing was
pulling her life force all the way through her body and
removing, or at least shrinking, any blocks that were
inhibiting the free flow of energy through her. All sickness,
he informed her, had a corresponding energy block.
Therefore, all people had within themselves, somewhere,
the power to assist their bodies to repair, no matter what the
affliction. Jane found this concept intriguing as it
empowered the individual. She had never thought about it
this way. In fact, she thought just the opposite. Jane was
eager to hear more, but Wong suggested that she needed to
take time to thoroughly understand and incorporate the new
information into her own life and body. Jane accepted that
and promised to practice her breathing every day. Wong
suggested she join a yoga class or learn Tai Chi, since both
disciplines were based on the concept of energy flow.

Meanwhile, Jane had been avoiding thinking about
her life and what she wanted to do, considering all that she

had discovered. She certainly wasn't going to let anyone tell her what to do anymore. But, she was a little overwhelmed by her options. While she was stewing in indecision, Fiona received a phone call from a friend who asked her if she could come back to the city for a while to help her take care of her sick mother.

Fiona wanted to go, but didn't want to leave Jane alone. Jane needed to decide what to do. Charles and Helen had been calling every day to see how she was, and to ask if she wanted to come home. Jane's anger at both of them persisted. She had no desire to see them, but this might be as good a time as any to face them. She needed to make it clear to them that they were never again going to run her life. Also she wanted all that was rightfully hers; control of her shares in the corporation and the blanket chest. She dreaded talking to Charles. But it must be done and she knew she could do it now.

The Confrontation ...

Jane's grip tightened on the steering wheel after she dropped Aunt Fiona off and started driving across the city to the house, that she had once called home, to see Charles, whom she had called father, papa, or dad for nearly twenty years. Her thoughts drifted to Helen, the woman Jane had thought was her mother, but with whom she had absolutely nothing in common. Finally, she knew why. This must be what adopted kids feel like, when they first find out, Jane reasoned, but she knew her experience was very different She wasn't chosen; she was dropped in their laps along with a lot of money. Well, truthfully even if she hadn't been found, they would still have had the money. And, to be fair, Charles had personally worked to multiply that money. No, more likely, he made sure he raised her so he could control the money. What other reason could there be? She would have been a lot happier with Fiona. She imagined that Fiona was probably a lot like her real mother. How she wished she could have known her real mother and father. Who was he anyway? Aunt Fiona told her that no one knew anything about him, really. His parents had both died when he was a child, and he had grown up with his grandparents. He didn't have any siblings so Jane figured there weren't any relatives from his side. It seemed odd to only come from one family.

A car honked and Jane realized she had drifted into the left lane. She had better pay more attention to her driving. She didn't like driving in the left lane because it was usually slower. Soon she would be through the busy traffic area and turn into her old neighborhood. She braked to avoid a car making a right turn in front of her, checked her left and pulled over quickly, but there was a car parked in her lane not far ahead, so she signaled right, and pulled back over in the faster lane. As she continued to battle traffic, Jane wondered what life was like on a sheep farm. There certainly would be no traffic jams and probably no silly society parties either. No, of course not, her real mother would not have been a socialite.

As Jane turned off the main street and into her old neighborhood, she noticed a house landscaped with trees and plants that reminded her of the rainforest. What would life have been like if she had been allowed to either stay with Narana or at least visit her? Narana had lived in the outback where the sheep farm had been, and in the rainforest. There was so much Jane could have learned from Narana, if they had had more time together. How Jane wished Narana were still alive so she could thank her for taking care of her.

Narana was the most significant person in Jane's life, and Jane knew nothing about her. Perhaps Daraha would tell her about Narana someday; if she could ever forgive Jane for the way she behaved. Jane prayed she would.

Here was her street. The houses were much larger, and set back away from the street at the end of long driveways. Just a few more houses, Jane took a deep breath. It was now or never. She really didn't want to do this. Charles' car was not in the driveway when she pulled in, though it was past time for him to be home. Fiona had called and told them when to expect her. He probably went to play golf to avoid seeing her. But as she climbed gingerly out of the Land Rover, and shut the door, she heard his car pull in behind her. She focused on taking a deep, long breath.

"Hello!" Charles welcomed her with a wave from the other side of his car. Before she could say anything, he had opened the back door, bent down, and popped back holding a beautiful orchid in full bloom.

"This is for you, I stopped and picked it out myself," he said proudly. Jane didn't know how to react. Her anger was somewhat deflated by his kind gesture.

"Thank you," she managed. She was saved by Helen who poked her head out the front door just then.

"Don't stand there in the driveway, come on in. I'll bet you are just exhausted after such a long drive." Helen continued chatting as they walked into the house. "How is your hip? Did you have any trouble with the traffic? It's always terrible this time of day. How about a nice cool drink? Jane, you go freshen up and I'll fix your favorite."

Jane stood there looking at Helen for a minute, still unable to think of what to say. She turned and walked upstairs to her room. Only it wasn't her room anymore; it never would be again. Everything was just as she had left it on her last visit. She went in the bathroom and splashed water on her face. Tears stung the backs of her eyes. It wasn't supposed to be like this. She was outraged because these people had done horrible things to her. She should hate them. How come she felt like this, such mixed emotions? She took a few of the healing breaths Wong had taught her and began to regain her control. It occurred to her that maybe, just maybe, they did love her and had thought their decision was best for her. After all, she had been very sick. She would make an effort not to be hurtful with her questions, but she absolutely did want some answers. Jane brushed her blonde hair, tucked her blouse in, and went downstairs.

The evening progressed smoothly. Both Charles and Helen hadn't looked too surprised when she called them by their first names. Fiona had probably warned them, Jane realized. Helen had fixed her favorite dinner, spring lamb with mint sauce and roasted potatoes. The conversation during dinner stayed on an even keel. Jane listened to her father answer her questions about what had happened. His story did not differ much from Fiona's. He said he always loved her and that she looked just like her mother, Mary, his favorite sister. He had looked after Mary when she was little, and was disappointed when she married and moved so far away. Charles said he regretted never getting around to visiting her during the three years she lived on the sheep station, but the demands of his business had kept him away.

Helen said very little, but sniffled more than once. She made a little joke about how difficult it is to swallow lamb; and they all laughed remembering the time Charles choked when Jane asked him about her childhood. Jane seized this congenial moment to tell them without rancor, how deeply she was hurt because they had never told her the truth.

Charles and Helen looked so crestfallen when she said this, that Jane nearly started to cry. Amazingly, she found herself not even needing to know why. It was suddenly obvious; they were being true to who they were and how they ran their lives. They had intended to keep her from harm but instead, they hurt her more.

Coffee, Australian champagne and chocolate covered strawberries were served on the veranda. Jane sipped on her champagne, her favorite after-dinner drink, and remembered her sixteenth birthday. She had been inexplicably unhappy. She mentioned this to Helen as she was about to bite into a strawberry.

Tears spilled down Helen's face as she laid the strawberry down, "I always tried so hard to make up for all that had happened to you and nothing I did worked." Jane choked back a sob herself. She hadn't ever thought of Helen this way. She had always seemed so shallow, with her social climbing and all. Jane stood up, walked over to Helen and hugged her. "I'm sorry, Mother, I just didn't understand." After a few more tears Jane let go and went back to her chair.

Jane turned to Charles who had been watching them quietly. "I would like to know about the business, please, I understand I own twenty percent of the company stock."

"Yes, technically that is true." Charles tone was defensive. Jane's back stiffened.

"What do you mean, technically?" She heard an accusatory tone in her voice.

"Well, as sole heir to Mary's estate, you did inherit the stock. But it is in a trust and I am the trustee. I manage your part of the business."

"Now that I'm of age, doesn't the trust revert to me?" Jane pressed.

"It will one day, but then you'll have to sign a new contract in order for your shares to be properly looked after." Charles' authoritarian tone was riling Jane.

"This is exactly how you have always talked to me. I won't sign any contract at all. I'm going to vote my own shares. Thank you very much." She rose as she was speaking and her voice rose with her. "I'd like to see the trust papers, now please," she demanded.

Charles stood and towered over her. "Come to my study and you can read them."

Jane followed him in and shut the door behind her. He removed a picture from the wall and started working the combination to the safe. Jane had never known there was a wall safe there. Charles shuffled through several papers, and handed the correct ones to her. Jane took them and sat down across from his desk to read. It didn't take long for her to realize that she had absolutely no control of her shares until she turned twenty-five or got married. She looked up and glared at Charles.

"I suppose you thought a man would know more about business and make better decisions than a girl would. Oh, my!" Jane's voice rose as she had a flash of insight; all those golf games. Bob was one of the boys. "So that's why you liked Bob so much. You can be certain, I'll turn twenty-five before I get married." Jane's voice was strained and her fingernails dug into the palms of her hands. "And I will have my lawyer see that my shares remain mine alone, not my husband's, no matter when or whom I marry." Jane felt very strong and certain about what she was setting forth as she had given it a lot of serious thought following her long discussions with Fiona about men controlling women's lives. Jane was determined to never to be in that position again. Moreover, she wanted some say in the decisions of the companies the family owned, especially regarding environmental issues.

Charles just sat gazing at her for some time. Finally he spoke, "It is more difficult than you think to run a multi-company corporation. One does have to have some business acumen and you have none." His voice was quiet, but sounded condescending to Jane.

Jane stood up from her chair, her eyes blazing at the man who presumed, because he had raised her, that he, and he alone, knew what was best. "I will learn what I need to know about business and you will *not* control me or my shares. Good night!" Jane tried to exit calmly. She gave a quick good-night smile to Helen who was nervously peering in from the veranda and then went upstairs to bed. When she collapsed on the bed at last, she was shaking all over and hadn't even noticed it until now. She waited until she stopped shaking, and got ready for bed. She purposely tried not to think. In her fury her thoughts were jumbled, which made her want to scream and pull her hair out. She brushed her hair with violent, jerky movements until she realized that the only person she was hurting now was herself. To collect herself, she concentrated on breathing. Soon the brush strokes became gentler and more rhythmic. Finally, she felt calm enough to crawl into bed. She curled up in a little ball; as she did it occurred to her that this was how she protected herself in her sleep. Well, at least this night was finally over and she had stood up to Charles for the first time ever. Jane started counting the length of each breath and eventually drifted off into a restless sleep.

The ship rocks back and forth ... she
feels nauseated ... she is clinging to a rope,

*desperately ... she is falling ... the waves
wash over her ... she screams ...everything
goes black.*

Disoriented, Jane tried to crawl out of the tightly
twisted covers but a shooting pain in her hip stopped her
short. She cried out. Helen came running into her room
where she found Jane drowning in tears. Helen put her arms
around Jane and stroked her head, until Jane gradually
relaxed. When she had gathered her composure, Jane
looked up gratefully at Helen, and made a request, "Could
you please just sit here with me for a while. My hip hurts
really bad." Helen nodded and continued stroking Jane's
brow. Jane fell back to sleep with her head in Helen's lap.

The next morning, Jane heard them talking in the hall,
before Helen poked her head in the door. "How are you this
morning, dear?" Her voice registered concern. Jane
summoned up a weak smile and said, "I'm better. Thank
you for staying with me last night. I'll get up now and come
down." Helen smiled and closed the door. The ache in
Jane's hip made getting up a challenge. After a hot shower,
a few stretches and some focused breathing exercises, Jane
felt better. She dressed and made her way down the hall,
noticing that the guest bedroom had been rearranged, and
the blanket chest was in a more prominent spot. Jane
walked in and knelt in front of it, running her hand lovingly
along the grain of the wood. It was as though she could feel
her mother, Mary, doing the same thing. She resolved to
take the chest back up north with her. But then she realized
she hadn't decided what to do. Wainton seemed like her
home now, so she guessed she would go back there, at least
for a while. She had a lot of unfinished business to take care
of there: her relationship with both Bob and Daraha, her job

and her friendship with Lucy. Yes, that was where she would go. She would have Charles help her load the chest in the Land Rover.

The Camping Trip ...

Jane drove down the red, red, sandy roads past wide, flat landscapes and little towns with silos. As she approached the park a group of emus ran away on strong legs, feathers bouncing. A flock of cockatoos took off screeching loudly. Suddenly, she remembered the details of a recent dream:

> *A flock of white cockatoos screeched overhead; several landed at her feet. She focused on the golden-yellow crest on the tops of their heads. The cockatoos strutted around, weaving patterns on the ground until she was hypnotized, one walked over and dropped a green leaf at her feet.*

Jane puzzled over the dream as she drove through the park gates and saw kangaroos everywhere. The colours were vivid in the fresh air after a recent storm and emotions rippled through her body. Jane had planned on staying in a nearby motel but as soon as she arrived at the park, she knew that she had to camp. She was glad she had loaded camping gear into the car before she left Wainton. She hadn't really thought she would need it, but here she was.

She realized she was just as angry as when she had set out to talk to Fiona. Charles was the most frustrating person she had ever met. Really, the nerve of him, telling her she couldn't have her great grandmother's chest, even though it had been left to her real mother and not to him. He had simply decided she would inherit it from him which infuriated her so much that she had screamed at him, and actually called him a bastard. Jane started to giggle, remembering the look of shock on his face. She'd fixed him. Then she had slammed out of the house, the last that she saw was Helen standing in the driveway crying. Jane did feel bad about that. Helen had been so loving to her last night. Jane hadn't wanted to hurt her, but Charles was too unreasonable. Jane took a deep breath. The same scene had been going over and over in her mind ever since she had got in the car, and somehow she needed to shift her thinking. Here she was now in this beautiful place and it was time to enjoy the present.

As she drove slowly on the unpaved roads, she passed several designated campsites, but none of them appealed to her. She saw what looked like a campground off the road to the right, so she turned in, driving across a deep ditch. Yes, there had been a campground here. It was a beautiful spot with giant stringybark trees, but there was no water supply. She'd have to carry water for washing up from the creek she'd passed back up the road. That was okay with Jane, she had a container of drinking water with her. This was perfect. It would be unlikely anyone else would bother to camp here. Most people preferred the designated camping areas. This national park was one of her favorites because you were allowed to camp anywhere so long as you followed the fire regulations. There had been plenty of rain and there were no restrictions, so she could build a fire if she made a safe fire pit. Jane set up camp quickly and gathered some dry wood for a fire. She liked hearing the birds sing and screech around her as she worked. Australia has the most beautiful birds, thought Jane proudly. She giggled because she had never been anywhere else and so she didn't really know. She was feeling so much better now. Just being in the forest was exactly what she needed.

After she ate the dinner she had cooked on the open fire, she went for a walk. It was nearly dusk so she headed for a nearby low hill. When she reached the top, the new moon was just starting to rise. She lay down in the soft grass and looked up at the stars which seemed to envelope her in an embrace. She lay for a long time, staring up, mesmerized by the magnificence of the universe. Finally, she stood up and raised her arms to the stars, giving a final farewell to the glittering night sky, before starting the trek down the hill to camp. As she looked up at the sky, she clearly saw herself in a mirror, her head and shoulders outlined by the stars in the Milky Way. It was as though her mystical or spiritual self, her eternal self, was in awe of her earthly self, just as she was by the heavens above. Her heavenly self seemed to say – I am a part of you, and you are part me.

In the morning, she took in a magnificent sunrise, and caught herself tapping her forehead as she stared at the beauty of the streaming colours. The tapping stirred something deep inside her. She experienced conflicting feelings of joy and sorrow, which brought back vague memories of her early childhood. Maybe she could ask Daraha to tell her more about that time. The thought of seeing Daraha brought up a lot of emotions. She wasn't sure how many more bouts of black moods she could handle. Jane shook her head as though to clear her thoughts, crawled out of her sleeping bag and decided to smile at the world. She took a deep breath. Her hip was stiff, but not too bad.

After eating some fresh fruit for breakfast, Jane set off on a brisk walk. She had covered some distance, when she came upon a place where the trees grew much closer together. Jane knelt down and touched the ground. It was warm and damp. The air here somehow smelled musty and fresh at the same time. Her hip had started to ache; it must be from the steep climb and then the downhill walk. She sat down with her back against a gum tree. She felt content and peaceful. She could breathe easier now. That is why she had come here. Occasional flashes of colour in the tree tops were all she could see as the birds played and sang, flying from one tree to another. Little sunshine penetrated the deep canopy of leaves. As Jane practiced breathing, she began to relax. She pretended to watch each breath of air come out of the ground and enter the bottom of her feet, flowing smoothly through each major joint: ankles, knees, hips. The intake of air continued as she pulled the breath up her back past her neck and around her head to her forehead. She held her breath for a moment and as she did she could see the most beautiful colour of purple. She let her breath out slowly, aware of it as it traveled backward on the same pathway. Each time Jane breathed this way, the joints in her hips relaxed, and the pain subsided.

Jane started to reflect on the hip pain. It seemed she always had it. When she was with Bob, it had occurred to her it was because she slept curled up in a ball. She had slept that way for as long as she could remember. The only time she could think of when she didn't hurt in the mornings was when she was camping. She usually awakened relaxed and rested when she was in the bush, or anywhere outside for that matter. Her body didn't feel as stiff and the ache in her hip was hardly noticeable even if she did sleep on the ground in her sleeping bag. She recalled her first camping trip with Pam. She had been an emotional wreck then too, but she remembered waking up in the morning feeling so alive.

That camping trip when she was only sixteen, was interesting in other ways, too. Her natural affinity for plants had been a surprise. It was as though she could intuit what the plants were thinking about, what they needed to grow strong and healthy. She even knew what their purpose was or at least some of the things for which each plant could be used. Jane shifted her attention to a plant growing at her side. She began experiencing it again. It was as though the plant was speaking to her, but of course it wasn't. Then she noticed its pink flowers with slender twining leaves, and partially exposed root. Jane felt an urge to taste it. With her fingers, she gently dug along the root to the end and broke it off, carefully covering the remaining root. She brushed the piece off, smelled it, and nibbled on one side. Why, it tasted like licorice, her favorite candy. How could she have sat down right by a plant that tasted like licorice? She looked at the plant with the tiny flowers and smiled gratefully. "Thank you," she whispered shyly. Jane rose from her position, sighed, and walked back down the path, chewing on the white root.

Chapter Eight

Back Up North

⑥　　⑥　　⑥

On her way through Wainton, Jane noticed several Aboriginal people carrying signs on the steps of the court-house. She slowed down, curious, since there hadn't been any demonstrations in this town that she remembered. One woman's face looked familiar … Jane realized with a start that it was Daraha. She whirled into a parking space and jumped out. As she started across the street, who should walk out of the courthouse, but Michael. Several men in the khaki-coloured uniforms of the Department of Natural Resources accompanied him. Jane stopped at the curb and Michael saw her. He excused himself, and went over to Jane.

"Jane, it's good to see you!" greeting her with a kiss. "How are you?"

"I'm much better now. I've lots to tell you and Lucy. As you know, it's all true, all of it and then some."

"I know," Michael said sympathetically, "Lucy has talked to Fiona several times and to Daraha also. Did you see Daraha over there? I think we both have some news for you." He motioned to Daraha, who was watching them from off to the side under a palm tree. When she walked over, Michael greeted her and asked if she would like to come with them to see Lucy. She looked anxiously at Jane.

Jane nodded and said, "Please come. I was on my way to see you to apologize for yelling at you and running out. I just had no idea what to believe."

Daraha smiled weakly and nodded. "I know, Lucy visit me and have letter from Fiona. They worry 'bout you."

Jane started to speak, but Michael put his arm around her and said, "We all have been very worried about you, including Bob."

Jane stared at Michael, when he mentioned Bob, but Michael didn't acknowledge it. He continued, "Come on, let's go to our place, Lucy will be dying to hear what has happened and she'll be mighty surprised to see you both," and with that, he started toward his car with Daraha following him. Jane dashed across the street and jumped in her Land Rover. Jane was so eager to get to Lucy's and hear all that had happened since she left that she nearly ran a stop sign on the way.

After many hugs and kisses and assurances to Lucy she was all right, and Jane's surprise at seeing Lucy's blossoming figure in the ninth month of her pregnancy, everyone had settled down to listen to Michael's story.

"Well," Michael began, "about those shots that were fired at you, Jane. We went out to the river mouth again. Only this time, two DNR boats hid upriver and a helicopter stayed just out of sight, waiting for us to radio. We didn't have to wait long. Shots were fired – they were fired from the shore, right near the mouth of the river. Some poachers were camping there, waiting for a boat to come to pick up their loot Apparently, they fired at us to scare us away. They had several bags of illegal game, including rare white possums, and golden-shouldered parrots. There was a lot of gunfire exchanged. I wasn't in any danger, but it was really exciting. The DNR caught three men, one strange, old, bearded guy and his two sons. The old guy was an odd one; he was wearing a cabbage palm leaf for a hat. He was quite mean, too. He was abusive toward his sons when they were caught and even today in court his sons seemed afraid of him."

As Daraha sat listening big tears ran down her face. Jane went over to comfort her, asking her what was wrong, and Daraha collapsed into her arms. "He's one who took you," she sobbed. "He kill Pero." Daraha started wailing with grief. Lucy sat little Mikey on the floor and rushed over to Daraha. Jane felt numb. She allowed Lucy to take over with Daraha and sat down on the floor herself to keep from falling. There was so much violence around her that she had trouble believing it all.

"Michael, what happened at the courthouse today?" Michael replied that it was merely an arraignment, the trial would be held later. The Aboriginals were there making sure this guy didn't get off. Apparently, he's been terrorizing their community for years. Even though they knew about his poaching, they were afraid to try to stop him because he had killed several of their men over the years. The murders had been reported to the authorities, but he was never charged. As Michael related this information, Daraha was moaning and rocking back and forth in her chair.

After a rather solemn dinner, Michael took Daraha home. Jane had wanted to go home, too, but decided not to when she learned that Bob had moved back in. When Jane thought about Bob, confusion reigned; she still loved him, but she wasn't sure she liked him. He not only had been unsupportive, but his attitude about her past was so negative. She still felt extremely uncomfortable when she thought about the scene when she threw him out. On the other hand, she didn't have any idea what she was going to do.

As Lucy and Jane went over everything that had occurred, Jane felt tears spring to her eyes. She wasn't very strong emotionally. Relieved, Jane accepted Lucy's invitation to stay with them for a few days while she sorted out her life.

The Reconciliation ...

A few days passed before Jane summoned enough courage to call Bob and arrange a meeting at the Tree House Cafe for dinner. When she saw him, she melted. She felt so warm and secure that she was sure they would be able to work things out. Bob immediately told her how sorry he was; he begged her forgiveness for not believing her when she told him about Daraha and her early life. Bob appeared surprised when he learned of her shares in the corporation, and agreed she should control the voting rights. After a tearful dinner and much sharing, Jane went home with Bob.

Everything seemed fine for a while. She and Bob spent a lot of time together: cooking dinners, playing tennis, and listening to music. Bob wasn't very happy when she went back to work for Michael, but he didn't complain or hold it against her. He seemed to understand that she needed to do some things her own way.

Jane was growing stronger. Her hip pain decreased from doing yoga twice a week, and using the breathing technique daily. She spent a fair amount of time with

Daraha and even volunteered at the Aboriginal Centre. She was shocked to learn that Daraha's children had been taken away from her after Narana's trial. That was a turning point: Jane decided that if Daraha was strong enough to face such huge losses in her life that Jane could do it too. Moreover, Jane vowed, she would always be there for Daraha. Bob had been fairly supportive of her new interest as long as she didn't go to the Aboriginal town at night. He still harbored some ridiculous ideas, but Jane tended to minimize them.

Jane began to think maybe she and Bob were finally ready to get married now and was delighted when Bob whisked her away to the nicest resort on the coast, wined and dined her for a week, and then offered her the diamond again. She was so happy, and felt in control of her own life for the first time. Even planning the wedding didn't seem to phase her. She decided it would be held at Aunt Fiona's beach house and that she would invite Charles and Helen to the celebration.

Then the trial began. Somehow the poacher must have had plenty of money, because he brought in one of the country's best criminal lawyers to represent him. Just before the trial started, Jane went in to give sworn evidence. The lawyer for the prosecution tried to use Jane's childhood memory of the poacher killing Pero as evidence, but the opposing lawyer made mincemeat of her, implying that her memories were just hysterical hallucinations. The poacher's lawyer had treated her so derisively that she left the office in tears.

When Daraha learned of Jane's experience, she became afraid that the poacher would be set free and would come after both Jane and her. Michael was called to give evidence in court, but Jane was not. She learned later that the lawyer for the prosecution felt she would be an unreliable witness based on her pre-trial performance.

Each day of the trial, which lasted several weeks, a few Aborigines stood outside the courthouse. Jane became more and more concerned about Daraha. Finally, she invited Daraha to come stay with her and Bob to make sure she was safe. Daraha was very grateful, and soon took over all the cooking and cleaning to help out. She even started baby-sitting for Lucy. Things seemed to be going fairly well, except Bob didn't come home in the evenings very much. He claimed he had to work late, but Lucy informed Jane that Bob was often out drinking at the local pub.

The trial finally came to an end. Much to the shock and anger of the Aboriginal community, the poacher was found not guilty on all charges except poaching protected species. He was saddled with a large fine but released from jail. His sons were also found guilty of poaching. They, too, were fined, but were not released from jail as they couldn't pay their fines. Naturally, the Aboriginal community reacted to the injustice with fury and terror. The talk of prejudice in the white court system caused the story to be picked up in *The Sunday Australian* and soon there were reporters swarming all over town. Jane and Daraha were interviewed by a woman reporter who acted as if she believed them and promised to tell their story truthfully, but Jane doubted it would ever be published.

The Sunday Australian ...

"Daraha, did you see this?" Jane burst through the door of Lucy's kitchen where Mikey was eating lunch and Daraha was warming a bottle for little Katrina.

"No way I see anything. Busy here, can't you see." Daraha smiled. That Jane, she was always excited about something. Daraha was enjoying feeling needed. She had been lonely for so long, not knowing what had become of her children, Possum and Oonta. They were adults now, like Jane. Daraha still ached for them, wondering if they were happy and if they had children of their own. She had so many questions and no answers. Maybe, like Jane, they didn't remember anything. Daraha didn't give up hope. They would find her. She believed they would come home someday which is why she never moved from her mother's little house until now. In the meantime, she took pleasure in her new life with Lucy and her children and her darling Jane. She would rather live with Jane, but that Bob. Daraha didn't want to cause problems so she had moved in with Lucy and Michael.

Jane stood in front of her, waving around a newspaper and trying to read it at the same time.

Daraha motioned her to a chair. "Sit down Jane. Calm down. I don't understand a word you saying 'cause you going too fast."

"That newspaper reporter we spoke with after the trial wrote this. She wrote about everything; Pero's death, the way I remembered it, Possum and Oonta being taken away, even about Narana walking all the way to the rainforest with me on her back. Can you believe it?"

Daraha sat down hard. No, she couldn't believe it. "Lemme see that." Jane handed over her part of the newspaper. There was a picture of her and Jane together in front of the courthouse.

"Oh, my gosh," Jane stood up and walked to the door and back, engrossed in what she was reading. "Here's a reprint of the original article from Narana's trial." Jane was weeping as she read. Then she sat down again. "I'm so sorry, Daraha. It must have been terrible for you and Narana. How I wish I could have thanked her. Uncle Harold was so foolish. I can't imagine what he was thinking when he accused Narana of kidnapping."

The phone rang. It was Lucy. She and Michael had stopped by the office after church and picked up *The Sunday Australian* on the way. She figured Jane was with Daraha.

"Please don't leave, Jane. We'll be home in fifteen minutes. This is just too wonderful." Lucy hung up.

Jane had just replaced the receiver when the phone rang again. It was Bob. "What the hell is going on? The phone is ringing off the hook for you! Some reporter just rang. Lucy rang. Your mother rang. And Fiona rang. You'd better come home now! And bring that newspaper with you. I want to see how much damage you've done now."

"Damage?" Jane retorted. "I didn't cause any damage. The damage was done to me and Narana and Daraha. Now, finally, it is being reported ... the truth this time."

"Yeah, well, we'll talk about that when you get home." Bob hung up abruptly.

Jane shrugged. "Not everyone is pleased by this article and he hasn't even read it yet. Well, I'd better call Fiona."

Before she could lift the phone, it rang again. It was Fiona. "Well, my dear, you have certainly caused some commotion this time around."

"What do you mean? Daraha and I just told the reporter the truth."

"Yes, I know you did, but have you read the part about Harold and Charles and the corporation? It's going to have repercussions."

"Oh, to hell with that," Jane said nonchalantly. "It's all true. Charles will just have to deal with it. He has plenty of PR people on staff."

"Jane, it may be more serious than you think. Bad press almost always hurts stock prices. I'll be talking to Charles to see if we can put a better perspective on it."

"Aunt Fiona, please. This article is important. Maybe Possum and Oonta will see it and come home to Daraha. Something good has to happen, especially since that horrible poacher got off scot-free again."

"I know you're right, Jane. I'm just so used to worrying about negative publicity, I hadn't really thought about the importance of the truth coming out. I believe Charles could put a positive spin on this."

Jane sighed. She did love Fiona, but honestly, did anyone in her family have any perspective? The door opened and Lucy arrived with Michael and talking to them and Fiona at the same time was impossible. She hung up, promising to call Fiona later. After some of the flurry settled down, Jane asked Michael if he thought the article would be negative press for the corporation.

"I'm not sure. It was a long time ago, but that line about Harold paying off the papers so there would be less coverage of the trial, that won't sit well with the public these days. It makes people wonder what else the corporation has covered up. It could cause Lawton-Starr to be carefully scrutinized. That wouldn't be so bad, except that a couple of the companies it owns do have some questionable environmental practices. This may be just the ticket for some group to get in and investigate."

Jane just looked at Michael. It amazed her that one little article about her life could suddenly cause such an uproar. She *had* always wanted those companies to change their practices. Charles would just have to deal with it. Besides all the ruckus would die down in a couple of weeks anyway.

She and Lucy were fixing lunch, when Jane remembered Bob. "Oh dear, I forgot! Bob is expecting me home; I have to go."

"Nonsense, we'll just call and invite him over." Lucy was saying when they heard a car in the drive. It was Bob.

Jane hurried to the door. "Hi! I was just calling you. Lucy invited us to lunch." Jane opened the door for him.

"Lunch! Do you realize what you have done? There are reporters everywhere. They've probably followed me here. Your father is beside himself; he's already called an emergency board meeting, with representatives from all the companies the corporation owns. You and I and Fiona must get down there. We'll fly down tonight."

"Bob, I really don't understand why there's so much fuss. Daraha and I just told the truth."

Bob gave Daraha a disgusted look. "I'm sure you don't," he replied sarcastically. "Remember the CD you bought with the songs about the sugar refinery? Well, that *is* about the company Harold and Charles owned when you were found. The public has always been suspicious about its environmental practices. Even though Charles doesn't own the company anymore, some people think that there may have been a major cover-up back then. Since it is obvious Harold had the newspapers in his pocket in those days, it's likely he may have suppressed more than just the poacher story. At least those are the types of questions that the reporters were firing at your family today. The board needs to set a strategy to prevent this from going any farther."

"I recognize the consequences," Jane said calmly, "but I'm not twenty-five yet, so I can't even vote. I don't know why I have to go."

"Jane, think! You caused this mess. And soon you will be twenty-five. You have stated your desire to vote. Well, you must learn to accept some responsibility. What better way, than to see the consequences of your own actions, and to learn how much work goes into putting out a fire like this."

"You know, Bob," Jane's voice had a high pitch, "I didn't cause this "mess" as you call it. I will not go and be chastised by my father or anyone else in front of the board. Charles is not my father, and he should have had more scruples when he was young. Then he wouldn't have this problem now, would he?" Jane was practically hysterical. Lucy came over and put her hand out to Jane, but Jane turned away. She felt really threatened. How could her family do this to her? Jane was the one who had been damaged by their actions, she and Daraha and Narana. She was so angry that she could feel the tears rolling to the surface.

Bob turned to leave. "I'll expect you at home in ten minutes, Jane. Don't bring Daraha! We will be leaving at four o'clock sharp." The door banged after him.

Jane stood there trembling. Daraha started to say something, but Jane shook her head. "No, Daraha, it's not your fault. I'm so sorry I dragged you all into all this." She looked around at Lucy and Michael and the kids. "I have to go now." She grabbed her keys and rushed out.

The Invitation ...

Jane spun the wheels of the Land Rover as she backed out of the driveway and turned recklessly onto the highway. She tried to concentrate on driving. Jane's chest started to hurt from holding back her tears so she exited off the highway, and started down a dirt road. She needed petrol and the signs indicated that there was a petrol station somewhere around here, but she drove for fifteen kilometers and still didn't see one. Finally, she saw the station ahead and pulled in. While the attendant filled the car, she bought coffee and a sandwich. A sign up ahead pointed to a national park so she headed there to calm down for a minute. Inside the lush rainforest park, she pulled over behind an old white car. As she sat on the side of the road attempting to eat her sandwich, she kept crying. To make things worse, her hip was aching again. She wrapped her arms around her knees and bawled. The tears kept coming. Every time she was about to stop crying, she thought of Bob, and tears puddled in her eyes all over again.

Out of nowhere, she felt a warm hand on her neck and jumped. Looking up, she saw an Aboriginal lady smiling broadly, wearing a khaki skirt, a white shirt and no shoes. The woman appeared to be older than Daraha, but it was difficult to tell. Why, it was the same lady she saw in the supermarket the other day. The woman had smiled and nodded at Jane as if she knew her. Jane suddenly was embarrassed. Not only did she look a mess, but she was crying so uncontrollably that the lady must think she was mad. Jane rubbed her eyes with the backs of her hands and stood up.

The Aboriginal lady continued to smile and introduced herself, "My name is Flora. You know Daraha, don't you?" When Jane nodded, Flora explained, "Daraha and I have known each other for a long time now. I am teaching her about medicinal plants of the rainforest. She helps me gather plants sometimes."

At the mention of Daraha, Jane burst into tears again. Daraha was the main reason she and Bob were fighting so

much. Bob got so angry with Jane when she asked Daraha
to come and stay with them. He was rude to Daraha right
from the start and he had stayed out most nights while she
was there. When Jane asked him if he could come home
more, he assured her it wouldn't happen until Daraha left.
Even after Daraha went to stay at Lucy's, it hadn't made
things any easier between them. Now, with her story in the
newspaper, Bob was impossible. Jane had embarrassed him.

Jane smiled bravely at Flora through her tears, then
turned to walk to the car. Flora followed her and said. "I
know you are in a lot of turmoil right now, but maybe it
would help if you could talk."

Flora paused, as Jane shook her head and started to
open the car door. Then she stated, "I am the grandmother
of many and the shoulder for many tears. I know I have
helped many problems, just by listening." She laid her hand
on Jane's arm and questioned her, "It's that boyfriend of
yours, right?"

Jane nodded, feeling Flora's hand resting on her arm
and smelling the musty odor of the earth. Jane instantly had
a flashback of another Aboriginal woman, one who looked
a lot like Daraha. Jane hiccuped and sighed, "I hope Daraha
didn't say anything she shouldn't have, about Bob and me."
Flora shook her head, and led Jane over to a log and handed
her a piece of root to chew on.

Jane bit into it and it tasted of licorice! "Hey, this is
my favorite. Where did you get this?"

Flora laughed, "The rainforest has many secrets and
gifts. Today I have been collecting some. I send them down
south to a company that dries the plants and distributes
them to health food stores." Flora handed her a cup of warm
sweet tea which Jane sipped gratefully. All of Jane's woes,
her whole life history started spilling out. After nearly two

hours, Jane began to feel guilty about taking up Flora's time. Hurriedly she thanked Flora for listening and said she must get going. She paused for a moment, wondering what had possessed her to tell a stranger everything about her life.

"Jane, I am not really a stranger to you." Flora said knowingly.

Jane jumped, "How'd you know what I was thinking?"

"Oh, I knew Narana when we were kids. She was my best friend. We were both learning about the rainforest from an old medicine woman, before we were taken away. We met again years later when Narana came back to the rainforest with you. You see, you knew me when you were very little. Narana and I were very happy to be together again. She knew plants, Jane. She could hear them talk to her, just like you can."

Jane looked quizzically at Flora, "I can't hear plants, Flora. What are you talking about?"

"Here, I'll show you. Close your eyes and concentrate, I'm going to hand you some plants and I want you to tell me about them."

Jane wanted to laugh, but she was also intrigued. I might as well give it a go, she thought, after all, she had found the licorice root twice before. Flora disappeared for a moment leaving Jane leaning against a gum tree, breathing deeply, letting the birdcalls relax her mind. She felt a seed placed in her palm, a hard seed with a soft casing at one end. She thought immediately of the crispness of an apple and said, "crisp." Next, a knobby root was placed in her hand, causing her mouth to flood with a ginger taste. Then, a soft leaf and stem made her think of watercress. She opened her eyes and Flora had laid them out side by side. The seed was jet-black with a scarlet fleshy jacket. She bit into the jacket and it was crisp, just as she had imagined. Next, she picked up the the root, which looked like any other root. She bit into it, and the taste of ginger rushed into her mouth exactly the same way as she had tasted in her imagination. The leaf, actually looked and tasted like watercress. Flora identified them as red-jacket, Queensland ginger and Australian watercress. Flora also taught her the Aboriginal names for the plants, which Jane found difficult to pronounce.

Jane looked at Flora in wonder. "I didn't know I could do that. Would you teach me more?"

"Yes, of course. But not today. It's getting late. Do you want to meet me here next week? We can go for a walk in the forest."

"Oh yes!" Jane was surprised at her own excitement. She grinned at Flora, who smiled broadly and nodded knowingly.

"Jane, Daraha will give you my phone number; call so we can set up a time. Until then...." Flora walked over to the old white car, got in and with a wave, drove away. It wasn't until Flora was out of sight, that it occurred to Jane to ask her what Flora meant about her and Narana being taken away. Surely they weren't taken away from their families, too. It was possible, Jane supposed. Flora's manner of speech was quite different from Daraha's and she didn't even have an accent. Perhaps Flora went to Uni. She would have to ask.

When Jane got home, Bob was already gone, as she was sure he would be. Ever since the merger with Blue Star and Bob's promotion, Charles had invited Bob to board meetings. Jane suspected Bob was being groomed for a higher position.

The answering machine was blinking. There were messages from several reporters requesting interviews; Lucy had called, worried as usual; and Helen had called. Jane decided to call her back.

"Mother," Jane pleaded when Helen picked up on the first ring.

"Oh, Jane, darling," Helen sounded relieved. "I've been so worried. Bob said no one knew where you went. You really must stop disappearing like that, you'll give me apoplexy."

"I'm sorry, Mother. I just couldn't stand being told what to do and that the whole mess was my fault. I didn't cause anything."

"I know you didn't, but your father just sees everything differently. Thank goodness Fiona came down with Bob. He flew to her place first, then they came here together. They're all in the meeting now. Don't worry, Fiona will help calm Charles down. She always does. Honestly, I can't reason with him when he gets like that. You always manage to upset him more than anyone else."

"I didn't do it on purpose. I hate fighting. When I gave the interview, I didn't even think about it actually getting published. And, anyway, we were only trying to tell what a terrible man the poacher is. We just told the truth."

"Darling, I know you didn't mean any harm. Try not to worry about it. Go on with your life. This will all work out. They're probably all up in arms over nothing. I'll keep you posted, I promise."

Jane was glad she had called Helen. She didn't want to worry her, and it was reassuring to know that Helen was not upset with her. She glanced at her watch. It was too late to call Lucy, she'd probably be in bed by now. Jane would see her at work tomorrow.

The Mountains ...

When Jane contacted Flora the following week, Flora asked if she would mind driving up into the high country for a walk in the mountains instead of in the lowlands. She explained that she surveyed endangered species of plants and animals for the Department of Natural Resources, and she needed to spend an afternoon and evening in the mountainous rainforest area north of Wainton. Jane was delighted to accompany her, since she had never been in that area. However, she was a little concerned about hiking up the mountain because of her bad hip. Flora assured her it wouldn't be a problem. They would drive up, and walk only a short distance. However, Flora warned that they would be out quite late because she needed to search for nocturnal wildlife. Bob was going to the city for a couple of days for another meeting so Jane didn't bother telling him she was going with Flora. She didn't want to deal with his disapproval again so soon. They hadn't talked much anyway, since he returned from the board meeting. His only comment was that he hoped Jane wouldn't create any more messes for the board to clean up. Jane's response was to put in extra hours for Michael so Bob worked late every night.

Flora and Jane started their long, but scenic drive right after lunch. The terrain changed as the low plains, covered with fields of sugar cane, gradually began to climb through rolling hills. Numerous small hobby farms dotted the land here which were owned by people who had relocated from the city, clearing only a few acres and building homes with trees growing all around. Several species of birds inhabited this area, Flora told Jane, along with the musky rat kangaroo, the smallest and most primitive kangaroo. Flora stopped the car along the road for a few minutes and sure enough two tiny kangaroos, which actually did look like giant rats, appeared in a clearing in the forest. Jane was delighted; she told Flora she had never had a guide before. Flora just laughed and told Jane she hadn't seen anything yet.

As the road became steeper with sharper curves, Jane experienced waves of motion sickness as a result of the car swaying back and forth. "Look behind you," Flora recommended to Jane. When she turned, she completely forgot her discomfort. "I had know idea we would be able to see the ocean," Jane said awestruck by the spectacular view.

"Oh, that's not your last view. We'll stop at a turnout a few miles up the way. Then you can see all the way down to Wainton and for miles along the coast. After that we'll go off the main road into a state preservation area where we'll have tea and wait for sundown. That is where the real excitement begins. Meanwhile, roll down your window and breathe a little fresh mountain air."

The rest of the drive, once they turned off the main road into the state forest, was bumpy and winding. Jane was quiet, letting Flora concentrate. Their conversation earlier had been interesting, with Flora explaining her views on energy. Actually, her description of energy fields was similar to Wong's, and Jane believed she grasped what they were talking about. She knew that she could tap into her own energy field and expand it with her breath. She had been practicing doing that in her yoga classes and via the breathing technique she had learned from Wong, which continued to help relieve her hip pain significantly. She was a little surprised when Flora explained that plants communicated to her through their energy fields and hers. Jane admittedly had never seen an energy field. She guessed that until she did, she probably would remain skeptical but the whole concept was interesting to explore and she wanted to learn more. After some time, Flora stopped the car near a clearing.

"We'll have tea here, and then after dark we'll sneak up the road farther to look for possums."

"Are they all we are looking for?" Jane puzzled aloud. "There are possums in the city park, too. They practically chase you for food."

"Yes, that is true." Flora smiled as she opened the car's rear door and retrieved two folding chairs and a picnic basket. "But the possums we are looking for here have very few places where they can survive. They are afraid of people and haven't been bred successfully in many zoos. The possums' habitat is shrinking rapidly, and soon they may become extinct. Each time we lose a species to extinction because people have invaded their habitat, I become extremely concerned. Someday, the same thing may happen to man. We need to learn how to live with all creatures, preserving areas to meet their needs. That is what this refuge area of the wet tropics represents. It is 900 meters above sea level and has one of the greatest diversities of both flora and fauna in Australia."

Flora grinned when she mentioned her namesake. "There are "living fossils" here which have survived climactic change, ice ages and volcanic activity, and they still live here on this mountaintop. If we're lucky, we will see some of the rarest mammals in the world here tonight." With that, Flora handed Jane a sandwich and a cup of hot tea. They both ate ravenously anticipating the evening's adventure.

Later, after dark, Flora and Jane walked slowly along with the low intensity spotlights shining in the trees and looked for the possums. As they searched, Jane asked, "Can you see energy fields after dark?"

Flora looked over at Jane and smiled. She peered back up into the trees and continued her search. It was difficult to walk, look for possums and carry on an in-depth conversation at the same time. Flora finally responded after several moments of silence. "Energy fields are filled with light and colours. They are the essence of the being they surround. The energy is on the inside as well as the outside and it is always present. Therefore, the energy can always be seen. It may not be seen, however, by me or by another person at any given time; it depends on the person's ability to concentrate and perceive the energy. So, you see, right now I've got all I can do to walk, talk, and look for possums. I really can't hold my focus enough to perceive energy fields too, but I still know they are there. I am also aware that my spiritual self sees what I am doing and is always helping and guiding me, like right now. See that possum." Flora stopped and held her light steady. Jane shined her light in the same place, looked closely; and then saw the eyes.

"What kind is it?" Jane whispered. "It's white, isn't it?"

"I believe it is a rare white possum; they exist only in a few places such as this."

Jane remembered that it was the same type of possum that the poachers had when they were caught at the river mouth. She started to say so, but Flora held her fingers up to her lips, so Jane turned back to watch the possum. They stood quietly for some minutes in awe as the possum walked along a skinny branch where it was joined by another possum. As the two played together, Jane became aware of the sounds and smells of the night, the great trees around her, the earth beneath her feet and the stars overhead. She felt a wave of peace enter her body and she became one with the universe. In that instant, she understood that she was part of the tiniest cellular creature on earth and part of the farthest star. She had been there when time began and she could see there was no end. The energy she was seeking to understand was a circle, the circle of Love and Eternity. It encompassed every living being, plants, birds, animals, man, the earth, trees, rocks....

They spotted several more species of possum that evening as well as a tree kangaroo. Jane was completely overwhelmed and spoke very little, even when Flora stopped the car suddenly as they were crossing a bridge. Flora pointed the spotlight on a platypus swimming in the creek. Each sighting of an animal that evening was a monumental spiritual experience for Jane. She was exhausted by the time Flora delivered her to her doorstep. She simply hugged Flora and whispered "Good night."

The Tree ...

The next day when Jane awoke, she felt rejuvenated. She stretched and realized her hip didn't hurt at all. She wasn't quite ready to face other people, so she decided to take the morning off and go for a walk in a nearby forest. She called Lucy to let her know that she wouldn't come to work until later, got dressed, packed a light lunch and headed out.

A warm breeze rippled through the leaves. Sunlight filtered down through the long, slender leaves of the stringy bark blue gum tree where Jane lay gazing up. Her vision was slightly unfocused and she thought she saw a different quality of light around the leaves. As she squinted to get a closer look, the light started to change colour. Jane took a

deep long breath and marveled at the beauty of it all.
Suddenly she gasped. She had just seen it. She had seen the
energy field around the leaves of the tree, just like Flora had
described it. She tried to see it again, but she couldn't. Had
she imagined it? Surely not. She started to breathe rhythmically again and focused on the beauty of the leaves, and as
she did the light appeared again. She really did see it. Flora
was right. As she lay there in a daze, Jane wondered if she
would be able to see the energy fields of other plants and
animals? Flora had told her that all living things had energy
fields around them; they were the templates for the matter
that we normally see. If this were so, would she be able to
see the energy fields around people, like Wong did?

These thoughts ran through her mind as she stared at
the beautiful colours surrounding the tree. The longer she
admired the energy field, the larger it grew. A cockatoo
screeched from a nearby tree. Jane turned her head to look,
and as she did she heard a voice, "Never forget when you
see a white cockatoo, something significant is happening in
your life."

Jane straightened up and looked around. No one was
there. The white cockatoo swooped down and landed on the
ground not two meters away. It cocked its head and looked
at Jane, then flew away. Jane looked up at the tree and
smiled.

The Visit …

Jane was cleaning the house, every nook and cranny.
She wanted everything to be perfect. This was the first time
Aunt Fiona had been to Wainton to visit. Jane had asked
Michael for the week off, had arranged for Daraha to come
for dinner one night and Lucy and Michael on another

night, so Lucy wouldn't need to get a baby sitter. Of course, Fiona would want to see Lucy's children at some point, especially Lucy's darling baby, Katrina, or little Kat as Michael fondly called her. There would be plenty of time for a visit or two during the days. Bob, too, seemed excited about Fiona's visit – he didn't know Daraha was coming over – as he liked her, and probably thought she would talk some sense into Jane about the corporate stock.

Jane had already talked to a lawyer and was making plans for a possible corporate takeover on her twenty-fifth birthday. As far as Bob knew she was working on getting control of her own stock, which he believed was reasonable. But he was adamantly against her desire to have a seat on the Board. The lawyer had assured her that takeovers of this nature were quite normal and, if she and Fiona joined together, their sixty percent would be sufficient to take control. However, he had warned her that sometimes corporate takeovers had a negative effect on the price of the corporation's stock. A takeover could possibly cause a large-scale dumping of their stock on the market, which might severely affect the corporation's ability to stay solvent, depending on the debt-to-asset ratio, the strength of the wholly owned subsidiaries, etc. etc.

Jane was hoping Fiona knew more about all this than she did. She had no idea what the financial status of the corporation was. At any rate, Jane's plan would only work if Aunt Fiona went along with it. The lawyer had encouraged Jane to think about what she would settle for if the takeover wasn't possible. Jane decided a seat on the board was the very least she would accept. Jane had also shared her strategies with Michael and Lucy, who were supportive and enthusiastic about her idea of having a more environmentally responsible corporate board. But Michael was uneasy about the takeover idea. He had cautioned her against it, suggesting it was far more difficult and dangerous than she imagined. She would see.

There, Jane thought as she put away the vacuum, the house looked great. The only thing left to do now was pick up some flowers and stop by the green grocers for some red capsicums and lettuce. Bob planned to grill a beef tenderloin and he liked roasted red capsicums with it. She would serve parsley potatoes and a salad, too. Oh yes, she also needed to pick up some more wine. They were sure going through a lot of wine lately. Drinking seemed to put Bob in a better mood. At least they had started spending some time together in the evenings, now that the uproar over her newspaper interview had settled down and Daraha was living at Lucy's. He hadn't been very happy about Jane's trips to the rainforest with Flora, but he figured out his objections did little good. Jane felt she needed to make sure Bob understood that he was not going to control her life, the way Charles had controlled Helen's and hers, when she was younger.

Jane had talked to Flora about it and her new friend had agreed that it wasn't good when one person controlled another, but she suggested that being controlled by another was possible only by some degree of consent. Jane totally disagreed. She had never consented to Charles controlling her, but he had anyway. Flora asked her to think about the Aboriginal people. She said the white man had done all sorts of things to control her people and, to the outside world, it looked as if it had worked. But Flora pointed out that real freedom existed on the inside. Perhaps the Aboriginals hadn't been controlled at all. Yes, many atrocities had been committed, and many people had suffered greatly. Today, the Aborigine live differently than their ancestors had for 50,000 years before them, that is true. And yes, Aboriginals have had to learn the white man's ways. Even more appalling, they still are not treated the same as the white man. However, the fact remains that the Aboriginal culture, their belief in their community, the value they place on the importance of their own existence, their respect for the earth and the stars, and the very essence of their being – their spirituality – is still intact, even after nearly a century and a half of invasion and domination. This is true freedom.

Jane couldn't comprehend what Flora was saying. She thought about it over and over, but it simply wasn't clear. She could say it, but she didn't really grasp its meaning. She felt she would never be free if someone else controlled any aspect of her life. She would take great pains to prevent that from happening.

The Fight ...

"What do you mean, you are planning to take over the board?" Bob made Jane jump when he angrily threw open the door and walked out onto the veranda where she and Fiona were standing.

"I didn't mean that exactly," Jane back-pedaled from her last statement. She hadn't heard Bob's car pull in the drive. "It's just that I'd like more say in corporate decisions. After all, I am one of the owners."

"Your father has built that corporation from the ground up, Jane, with all due respect to Harold." Bob acknowledged Fiona and nodded a brief hello. "Charles works very hard and is, I might add, very successfully making astute business decisions to encourage corporate growth. You, Jane, have no idea what that takes. You'd go in there thinking only of your high and mighty environ-mental ideals and screw the corporation up for good, like you nearly did with that damned newspaper interview. In no time at all, the companies would all go bankrupt. I simply will *not* allow you to even entertain such a plan, let alone carry it through." Bob commanded loudly.

Jane stood, drink in hand, with her mouth open. He was just like her father, she thought, just as Lucy had told her years ago. Why hadn't she seen it?

"Just what makes you think you can tell me what to do?" Jane inquired icily.

"If you are going to be my wife, you will do as I say on matters of business and that is that." Bob had drawn himself up to his full height as he spoke and was glaring down at Jane.

Jane felt her energy slipping away. Her knees felt weak, and a wave of anxiety flashed through her stomach almost to the point of nausea. She drew in her breath sharply and tried to maintain her composure. He was forcing her hand and she didn't feel strong enough to stand up to him. Jane looked to Fiona for support, but Fiona's eyes were slightly out of focus as she observed the two of them. Unable to get Fiona to respond to her pleading glance, Jane instead took a drink and tried to calm herself. Suddenly a feeling of rage shot through her and she squeezed the glass in her hand so tightly it broke. Jane watched, transfixed, as the blood mixed with the alcohol from her drink and dripped onto the tile at her feet. She opened her hand and the remaining pieces of glass hit the floor and shattered.

"What the Hell!" Bob roared at her. Fiona grabbed a towel from the tray on the table and wrapped Jane's hand. Jane was trembling and nearly fell into the chair Fiona pulled over for her.

Fiona looked up at Bob as she tended Jane's hand and said, "I think you should go for a walk."

Bob glared at her. "No way! I want to know exactly what is going on here. What is the meaning of *this*, Jane?"

Jane looked at him and then at her hand and started to cry. Bob stood staring at her for a moment, turned and left the house.

Fiona let out a sigh of relief. The energy exchange she had just witnessed had taken her by surprise. She usually didn't see energy fields around people so easily. This time it happened automatically. Perhaps she had observed their fields because she had put herself in neutral as she listened to Jane's ideas about the takeover. She hadn't wanted to be influenced by Jane's ideas or emotions. Instead, she wanted to hear her out and serve as Jane's guide or teacher as the younger woman examined who she was; what her goals in her life were; and how she was going to achieve those goals. Then, when Bob came out onto the veranda, Fiona had been taken aback by the enormity of his energy field. In his presence, Jane's energy field had immediately shrunk. As they carried on their conversation, arrows of energy shot out at the other one, piercing the other's field and taking energy Finally, Bob pulled most of the energy his way and Jane's energy field was depleted. It had been an incredible experience to watch the exchange. Now Fiona felt her job was to teach Jane to replenish her own energy field. Perhaps she should try to explain to Jane what had happened in energy terms between her and Bob; if she wanted to know.

Fiona applied ice to Jane's hand and said, "Please try to take some deep breaths, Jane, see if you can follow your breath. That's it. Now breathe into your hand. Concentrate.... Good.... Now take another breath ... pull it all the way through your body. Hold it at your forehead....

Yes. Your energy field is starting to replenish. Breathe out slowly."

Jane stopped crying and concentrated on her breathing. She sent energy to her hand with each breath. After a few minutes, she felt better and peeked under the towel at her hand. "Oh!" she moaned, "I didn't mean to hurt myself."

Fiona patted her head and said, "I know you didn't. I think it was a way for your body to show you how much it is hurt when you allow your energy field to be depleted like that."

"What do you mean?" Jane asked in a little voice.

"Well, I can explain on the way to the doctor's. I believe this needs some stitches and we should make sure there aren't any ligaments cut."

As they drove to the clinic, Fiona revealed to Jane what she had observed. Jane listened intently, while practicing deep breathing to stay calm.

But, Aunt Fiona," Jane interrupted, "you're saying I allowed my energy field to be depleted. I didn't. Bob attacked me and sucked my energy away to fill himself."

"Not exactly, Jane. You were attacking him, too, and attempting to fill yourself with his energy."

"Really? That's hard to believe. How could I? I just remember feeling completely overwhelmed when I realized he was just like Charles. I'm sure that's when he took my energy."

"No. That's when you went after his energy. Your energy field literally went up over top of him and shot out arrows around his head. Then he, almost in self-defense, shot an arrow out at your solar plexus area and started to draw your energy. Actually, I think if you hadn't attacked him, you wouldn't have been vulnerable to his attack."

"You mean, by attacking him, I agreed to his taking my energy?"

"No, what I mean is that you engaged in the same behavior as he, which literally forced one of you to "win." In other words, one of you would be able to walk away filled with the other's energy and feel "in control." Only this time, you stopped the energy drain by injuring your hand, which shocked and confused Bob, so he no longer felt stronger taking your energy. I suspect, in the past, you may have started crying, which probably elicited his sympathy and put you back in control because you started pulling energy away from him and back to you."

"Wow!" Jane reflected on Fiona's words as they pulled into the clinic. "I'll have to think about this."

"Don't forget to breathe into your hand to help it heal faster," Fiona reminded her as she opened the door of the clinic for Jane. Once you are checked in, I'll wait across the street in the park."

Fiona sat on the bench under a palm tree and watched as rosellas flew around the bushes and trees. She was aware that someone had been with her helping her serve as Jane's guide in this current situation and the entire episode was a turning point in both hers and Jane's lives.

When Jane came out of the clinic, she saw Fiona across the street and waved as she came over. "Everything is okay. I didn't cut any ligaments and I only needed a few stitches. I think it looked worse than it is." Jane displayed her bandaged hand. "I won't be able to type or wash dishes for a while though."

"How nice for you," Fiona said smiling. Jane giggled.

"I have kind of made a mess of your visit so far, sorry. I hope everything is better from now on," Jane paused. "I've been thinking about energy fields. I saw the energy around the leaves on a tree the other day. My friend Flora, who is teaching me about plants, sees energy fields all the time. Maybe we could all get together, there is so much I want to learn." Jane went on to tell her about everything Flora had taught her. Fiona sat listening and observing her.

"You're watching my energy field now aren't you?" Jane asked suddenly. "What is it doing? Can you see it all the time?"

Fiona laughed. "It's sparkling. And no, normally I don't see energy fields, but maybe I will from now on. I would like to meet Flora. I think it would be fun for us all to get together. Is she Aboriginal?"

"Yes, how did you know?" Jane asked, trying to think if she had given any indication of who Flora actually was.

"I'm not sure. When you spoke of her, I saw an older Aboriginal lady with a pleasant face and no shoes."

"That's her. She never wears shoes. She walks through the rainforest with no shoes on and never winces. She told me it helps her keep in touch with the earth. She is very well educated, too. She knows the scientific names for all the plants as well as the common names we use, *and* the Aboriginal names. She knows which plants we use for various medicines and other chemicals, which plants are edible, and the ways the Aboriginals have used plants for centuries that we haven't even discovered yet. It's pretty incredible."

"Jane, you appear to light up when you talk about plants. They must be significant to you. Perhaps you are on the verge of finding your life purpose."

"My life purpose? What do you mean?" Jane was intrigued. She had been trying to figure out why she was attracted to plants.

"I believe that each of us comes into this world with a certain mission, which we plan to accomplish during our lifetime. Sometimes discovering our mission is quite difficult, although we get many messages about it throughout our lives. The trick is to recognize the messages and follow them. It's easy to get confused about what the messages mean and go off in a different direction. Besides, we often get waylaid by life's little dramas and miss finding our purpose or life mission altogether."

"Really! I've never thought about life like that before. Have you always thought this way?"

"No, I've learned a lot recently. You know that I've traveled quite a bit and taken many classes over the past few years. After Harold died, I realized something was missing in my life. The most interesting part was that it had been missing when Harold was alive. So, I started examining my life and my place in the world. My explorations included studying cultures and religions different from my own. I discovered that there were common themes or truths, among all cultures and religions. People's lives and values are pretty much the same no matter where they live or how rich or poor their worlds are. As I continued my explorations, I began to experience a deep spiritual sense of belonging everywhere to everyone at the same time. Maybe a better way to describe it is a sense of kinship to everything in the universe. It is like I am a part of everything; the sea, the earth, the stars, the people, even the rocks and trees and plants."

"Oh, my gosh! Aunt Fiona, I had a very similar experience the other night when I was in the mountains with Flora. I had such a sense of connection with everything."

"That's it exactly. I thought you would understand. I call that sense of connection, consciousness."

"Is that why you can see energy fields, because you are conscious?" Jane wanted to know.

"Why yes, I believe it is." Fiona smiled. She hadn't thought of it that way before. "You know, Jane, I can honestly say that as I continue my learning, and expand my conscious awareness of my own spirituality, I am enveloped by joy. It's miraculous for me." Fiona stood as if to go, and offered Jane her hand.

The Phone Call ...

Daraha was washing up the breakfast dishes, after finally getting the children to go down for a late morning nap. Everything was hectic in this household today. Michael had to catch an early flight to the city for a meeting with some politicians about the impact of toxic sediment on the Great Barrier Reef. He had to have his shirt ironed and no one had mentioned it the night before. Lucy was frantic that Kat had a doctor's appointment that afternoon and she wouldn't be able to leave the office with Michael gone. Jane was nowhere to be found as usual. She was always going off to the rainforest with Flora, and now Fiona was going too. Then the phone rang.

"Hello?" Daraha answered cautiously. She wasn't accustomed to answering the phone yet. It rarely rang when she was there alone.

"Mum, that you? Daraha, that you?" A male voice inquired incredulously.

Daraha sat down. She couldn't think. It couldn't be. Was it possible?

"Mum. Possum here. Don't be mad at me, Mum. I didn't know where you are. Then, I read bout us in paper. Please don't be mad."

"I'm not mad. I'm,..." Daraha couldn't seem to get her breath. "Just give me time." She took a deep breath before breaking into a gentle sob. "Oh Possum, that really you? Where you? Oh my!" She was shaking and nearly dropped the phone.

"Yes, Mum it's me. You okay? Anyone there with you? I should have written you first, but once decided to find you, couldn't wait. I thought you dead. That's what they told to me."

"Possum, my baby. Ah, thank the ancestors! You finally coming back. Where you? You coming home? When? Not dreaming, talking to you, aren't I?" Daraha was so excited, she wasn't making any sense.

Possum laughed a big hearty laugh. "Oh Mum, it's great to hear you. I'm in Melbourne and an artist. You know, paint rainforest. I want to come see you. Do you have sleeping place for me? I haven't got much money."

"Jane will help. She always takes care of me now. She is real nice. Do you remember her?" Daraha realized that maybe Possum wouldn't remember. He was very young when Jane was taken away.

"Yeah, I remember. She caused a mob of problems. I don't want her looking after me." Possum sounded angry.

Daraha bit her lip. "Listen, Possum. You stay at Narana's house. I still have it. I stayed there all these years, maybe you and Oonta come find me. Please don't be mad." Daraha pleaded. "I don't think I could stand you being mad."

"Okay, Mum. I'm not mad. I'll try to come up next week if can get a ride. One of my mates drives a truck and he said could go to Sydney with him. Then find another ride. I'll let you know."

After Possum hung up, Daraha just sat there by the phone. She must have stayed there for a long time, because, when she heard Mikey playing in his room, she glanced at the clock, and it was nearly lunchtime. She'd better get busy. Lucy would come home for lunch soon. She wondered who would be taking Kat to the doctor. The phone rang again. Daraha answered hesitantly. It was Lucy. Her mother would be coming by to take Kat to the doctor and Lucy wouldn't be home for lunch. Daraha was relieved and disappointed at the same time. She wanted to tell someone about her son, but this way she would have more time to think about Possum's homecoming.

Chapter Nine

The Secret

    ⓖ   ⓖ   ⓖ

"Hello! This is Peg Wild from *The Sunday Australian,* business section. I'd like to ask you a few questions, please."

"I'm sorry, Miss Wild, but I've already sent my statement to the press. You will have to make do with that." Charles was irritated. How did this woman get his private number at the office?

"These questions are not about you and your current corporation now. They are about the sugar refinery you and Harold Starr sold eighteen years ago."

"That's all history. All relevant information regarding that sale is a matter of public record.

"Actually sir, we've uncovered some things that are not part of he public record, things I believe you will find extremely interesting. I would like to sit down with you and discuss it before we run the story. You have every right to make a comment first."

Charles was thrown off. The woman sounded sincere and not vindictive. He honestly had no idea what she was talking about. There had been violations, sure, regarding their use of chemicals that caused pollution, but they'd paid the fines. The entire sale had been above board and legitimate. Perhaps he should find out what she was talking about. After a moment of musing, Charles responded, "Yes, I will meet with you, Miss Wild. Lunch tomorrow at the Kangaroo Paw, say 1:30?"

"That will be fine. Until then."

Charles sat quietly at his desk. What on earth was this reporter trying to dig up? No one here now was with the company then. The only people who could know anything were Fiona and Gary London, who had purchased Big Reef Refinery from him and Harold. Gary had been a close friend of Harold's and they had even done some other business dealings together. Now, Gary and Charles were golfing buddies, but had no business connection. Gary was always a bit too slick for Charles' taste, and lots of Gary's company's environmental polices were questionable to say the least. Charles reflected back on the time when Jane had participated in that demonstration against Gary's refinery. Charles knew, in his heart, that she was right, but he had been furious that she hadn't talked to him first. A person in her position couldn't just go off willy nilly making accusations without understanding the consequences. And those interviews Jane had given that other reporter from *The Sunday Australian*. He supposed this new article was directly related to the last one, though Miss Wild claimed to be from the business section of the paper. One never knew when an investigative reporter would turn dangerous. He'd better give Fiona and

Gary a call to see if they could possibly think of anything this woman could've dug up.

One Hour Later ...

Charles was puzzled. Fiona had no idea what was going on. She was still visiting Jane and said there had been nothing in the news about the refinery since she'd been there. She asked Jane, who confirmed that it had been over a year since the refinery had gotten any bad press, and then it was about poor working conditions. Jane and Fiona had promised to make some inquiries and call back.

Gary London, on the other hand, had been a little nervous and evasive. He said he couldn't think of a thing about the sale and assured Charles he hadn't been contacted by anyone, but he insisted they meet for a drink tomorrow after the luncheon. Charles agreed to meet him at The Chess Club, a businessmen's private club where they both were active members, so their meeting would appear accidental.

Charles felt nervous as he entered the Kangaroo Paw and prepared to meet Miss Wild. He gave his name to the Maitre d'. Fiona and Jane had no further useful information, but promised to send him "energy" whatever the hell that meant! He followed the Maitre d' to a table by the window, where a young Aboriginal woman sat. She was dressed in a tailored suit with her curly hair pulled back tight away from her face. She looked to be Jane's age, and was light-skinned and attractive. Charles was surprised and must have looked uncomfortable, because the woman stood and extended her hand.

"I'm Peg Wild. I suspect you didn't realize over the phone that I'm Aboriginal. Most people don't because I don't have an accent"

Charles nodded as he sat down. He didn't like being caught off guard like this. They chatted briefly and ordered light lunches. Peg volunteered that she'd been placed in a wealthy family and well educated at private schools, where she learned perfect diction and where her heritage was completely erased. She'd attended University and traveled around the United States and Europe. She seemed pleasant enough to Charles. He mentioned that he had taken off little time for travel himself, as he was always working. When they'd been served their food, Charles asked her what questions she had about the refinery.

Peg reached for her briefcase and pulled out a file with Harold Starr's name on it and handed it to Charles. On top were the headlines about Harold's death, and how his parachute hadn't opened in time. Highlighted in pink was a short paragraph where the investigator stated that he could find no reason why the parachute hadn't opened. He said the ripcord had not been pulled. Charles vaguely remembered this, but everyone had ruled out suicide as a possibility at the time. Obviously this young lady wanted to bring out this possibility.

"Now look here, Miss Wild, Harold didn't commit suicide. He had no reason to."

Peg reached over and turned to another page in the file. It appeared to be an affidavit of some sort. Charles scanned it quickly. Some elderly Aboriginal man was claiming that his entire family of twenty-five people was shot and killed by a white man, who wore a cabbage palm hat. Evidently, the family had left the reserve and was living on property owned by the refinery, which they claimed to be their sacred home. This massacre reportedly happened eighteen years ago. Charles swallowed as he realized this might have occurred while he and Harold still owned the refinery. Even more coincidental was the insinuation that the same man who had just been tried for poaching in Wainton and who had brought Jane to Harold also committed this atrocity. Surely it wasn't true. Charles took his handkerchief out of his pocket and wiped his brow.

"Is there proof of this?" he asked in a subdued voice.

"No, not yet. But when this is published, I hope the authorities will search for the family's remains. It would make a good case against the poacher, don't you think?" Peg spoke with no trace of animosity in her voice.

Charles looked at her, "What is your connection to this? Was this your family?"

"No!" she replied curtly, "Let's just say I have my reasons."

"Is there more?" Charles asked reluctantly.

"You tell me. Did you and Harold pay the poacher to get rid of those people?"

"Oh, surely not." A wave of agony passed through Charles and he suddenly felt as if he were going to pass out. He put his head down in his hands trying to hold himself up.

Peg motioned for the waiter. "I think Mr. Lawton needs some assistance." She picked up the file, put it in her briefcase and left.

It was a while before Charles could collect himself. He tried to act as if nothing was wrong, but wasn't sure he had succeeded. He asked the Maitre d' to call him a taxi and managed to return safely to his office.

How could Harold have done such a thing? It was inconceivable. And yet it must be true. Jane will never forgive me, Charles thought, she will assume I was in on it. But he never imagined.... All he had ever wanted to do was to make up to Jane for her mother's death. He still felt guilty about not taking care of Mary. He was too occupied, letting himself be seduced by money, status and power. What, and how, was he going to tell Fiona? Surely she didn't know. It occurred to Charles that Harold had taken the easy way out. The bastard! Rage took over. What the hell had Harold done? And why? Did London know about this? Is that why he was being so evasive on the phone? The anger gave Charles strength. He glanced at his watch; it was time to confront Gary.

❻ ❻ ❻

That evening, Charles sat alone in his study. He had avoided Helen's questions at dinner. He wanted to tell her the truth, but he didn't think he could deal with her emotions. London was such a bastard. He'd known all along. He confided that he had told Harold he would refuse to buy the refinery with the Aboriginals on the property. So Harold had asked the same man who had brought Jane home to get those people to leave. Well, the poacher did, all right. Then he made Harold pay, a blackmail of sorts. The poacher was put on salary at the refinery after Harold bailed out. Gary had kept a lid on the poacher by threatening suicide himself. London had looked Charles directly in the eye and suggested he was perfectly willing to leave Charles holding the bag, also. Charles was in shock. He couldn't believe he had been so totally naive.

Now he had to summon the courage to call Fiona. Perhaps, he should fly up there. No, it would be better if he told her here. He would ask Fiona and Jane to come see him immediately. The news could be in the morning paper. Maybe it wouldn't break till Sunday, but he couldn't risk it. What to do about Bob was the next question. He had heard Jane and Bob weren't speaking and that Bob was staying at a friend's. Maybe it would be best to just leave Bob up to

Jane. But Charles felt he needed an ally and Bob had always been a strong one. Bob was a lot like him. In fact, Charles realized, that was probably why he and Jane weren't getting along.

Oh, God! The agony of telling them. Charles began to feel weak again. He laid his head down on his desk and began to sob. He wasn't aware when Helen came into his study, just that he took comfort in her arms. She sat stroking his head until he recovered enough to tell her what had happened. Amazingly, her reaction was calm. She called Jane and explained there was an emergency and asked her and Fiona to please fly straight here. She called Charles' office and had the company jet sent up north to get them. Next, she called the corporate lawyer and the corporate vice-president for public relations and asked them both to come to the house at six o'clock the next morning and to schedule an emergency board meeting for eight. She arranged for a driver to go to the airport and pick up Fiona and Jane. When she had done everything she could think of, she brought Charles some chamomile tea and sat on the footstool beside his chair.

"Darling, I know you didn't know anything about this. We will get through this. You didn't do anything wrong. We will try, however, to find a way to make up for this horrible atrocity. Whatever it takes, I will be at your side." She took Charles' hand and held it to her cheek, crying softly.

It was after midnight when Jane and Fiona arrived. Helen had tea ready and went to wake Charles who had fallen asleep in the study from sheer exhaustion. For the first time in their marriage, Helen was the one to speak. She asked everyone, especially Jane to remain calm.

She explained the entire sequence of events as best she could. There was something in the way Helen talked that helped everyone to absorb what had happened without jumping to conclusions and placing blame. Jane found herself breathing slowly and working to remain centered and focused. She realized she did not want to make the situation any worse than it already was. She felt a strange agony inside her, a grief for all of Australia, for oppressed people everywhere, and, somehow, for the oppressors.

The Offer ...

Michael ran his hand through his sandy hair. He was in a daze. The conversation with Jane was both shocking and terribly exciting. He pushed his chair back from his desk and stood up. There was no time to sit and think, he knew he wanted to do this. Of course, there were many factors to consider ... it would cause a major change in his and Lucy's lives. Perhaps, she would want to stay here and run their business. She knew it as well as he did and sometimes he felt she could run it better. Of course she didn't have the post-graduate degree he had, but she studied hard and kept up to date. Whatever Lucy wanted to do, they would find a way to work it out. Jane had insisted that Lucy come down for the discussions tomorrow, too. She knew they always made all their decisions together. He took a deep breath; he'd better go tell her.

Lucy was at a field station, reviewing an analysis and checking data for discrepancies, when she saw Michael drive up. She wondered what he was doing out here; she was supposed to meet him back at the office in an hour. She knew something was up as soon as she saw his expression.

"Let's put this analysis away for the day," Michael suggested after he'd greeted her. "We need to talk and I thought it would be better out here in the forest than in town or at home."

Lucy felt uneasy. Michael seemed so serious and direct. She quickly wrapped up, organized the data and signed off on the computer. She picked up her hat and said, "Why don't you grab a bottle of water and we can go for a walk."

As soon as they headed down the track, Michael started talking. He told her the whole story of the refinery, the Aboriginals, the poacher and Harold's suicide.

Lucy felt tears running down her checks. "Poor Jane and Fiona. Oh dear, and we shall have to tell Daraha. Jane's family has really had a rough time. You'd think that all that money would insulate you, but it doesn't. It creates the problems. Does Jane think Charles and Fiona knew about the massacre?"

"No, Jane's sure they didn't. She said Charles still isn't functioning normally. Also, believe it or not, Helen has stepped in, taking the lead and making all the decisions. Apparently, Charles is simply going along with her. Jane sounded like she really felt sorry for him. She said she thinks his whole world has been destroyed."

"Oh God, I bet! How is Fiona doing?"

"Jane said she is doing all right, but is probably in shock. Fiona is the one who came up with this great idea."

"What idea?" Lucy stopped in her tracks. Suddenly she realized there was more news Michael had come out here to talk to her.

"Well," Michael hesitated. "They have decided to make some major policy changes at the Lawton-Starr Corporation. First, all the companies they hold will be required to review employment and compensation packages to make sure all Aboriginal employees are being equally and fairly compensated. Future hiring will mandatorily seek qualified Aboriginals to fill new positions, until there is a more equitable representation at all levels of the companies. Fiona herself will oversee this effort."

"Great!" Lucy broke in. "Fiona was just talking about how important she thought that was the other day. She needs to feel she is contributing, and I think being involved will help her work through the pain of this tragedy."

"Yes," Michael agreed. "That is what Jane thought also." He walked in silence for a few steps, then continued. "The second part affects us."

Lucy looked at Michael, she could tell he was excited if somewhat apprehensive. "Go on," she said, sitting down on a log. "I'm ready."

Michael paced back and forth in front of her. Finally, he spoke. "They want us to come down tomorrow to discuss developing a new corporate policy which would govern the environmental impact of the various companies they hold. Jane suggested it might take the form of something like Fiona's new position, meaning that it would involve overseeing the policies and actions of each company in regards to its impact on the environment. Getting involved in this would mean a drastic change in our lives, Lucy. I don't know if we both would work for them, or only me, or if we could work on a consulting basis, and still keep our company here.

"But at the very least, it would involve a lot of of traveling to all of their companies on a regular basis. It could represent an extremely important development in Australian business practices. Jane says that each company's practices will be changed until they are having a positive, rather than a negative, impact on the environment."

"It's too bad they don't still own the refinery," Lucy said dryly.

Michael looked directly at her. "So, what do you think? Are you interested in doing this?"

"Of course I am, Michael! This is an amazing opportunity to lead Australian companies to a positive future, environmentally speaking. The impact will be greater than all the community panels and regulatory agencies combined, if we can find ways for them to handle the changes economically. Gosh, it'll be the most phenomenal change in Australia since the English arrived!" Lucy laughed giddily.

"Lucy, you're stretching it a bit!" Michael got a kick out of her boundless enthusiasm. "But I'm glad you agree with me. I was worried what you would think about moving our business and our family.

Lucy reached up and hugged Michael. "Whatever we need to do, we do. The only thing I want is to be personally involved, as part of the team. For the short time I stayed home after Kat was born, I was miserable. I need and want to care for our children, but I also need to be actively involved in environmental work. I've known that since I was a little girl."

Michael smiled broadly. "I know, that's why I married you. We're a team and that's how we will present ourselves at the meeting tomorrow." He looked up at the sun and noted that it was afternoon. They should start heading back. "I won't be able to tell the time from looking up inside an office building! We'll notice a lot of changes in our lives. It may not be easy."

"Yes, I know. It will take time, effort and lots of organization, but I'm ready to do it." Lucy sounded confident.

Michael felt tears in his eyes. He reached out and pulled Lucy close. "I'm so lucky," he murmured into the top of her head. After a few moments, he added. "They are sending a plane for us at eight o'clock tomorrow morning; we have a lot to do. We'd better get a move on." With that, he took Lucy's hand and they walked back together.

After they made arrangements to be away from the office for a few days, Lucy and Michael went home together planning to tell Daraha everything. When they arrived, Lucy's mother's car was in the driveway. Hurrying inside, they found Lucy's mom fixing tea and the children playing on the floor.

"Mom! What's up ? Where's Daraha?" Lucy inquired picking up Kat giving her a kiss.

"Well, something is up and *you're* supposed to explain it to me. Jane just called me long distance and asked if I would relieve Daraha. She alerted me that I might need to keep the children for a few days if Daraha didn't come back. After I got here, Flora arrived and Daraha left with her. That's all I know."

"Oh Mom, I'm sorry for all the confusion. Thanks so much for coming. I suppose Daraha was really upset. I'll have to call Flora later. We do need to fly down to see Jane probably for a couple of days. I hate to impose on you, but...."

"Don't be silly. Of course, I'm happy to do whatever you need, but would someone please tell me what is going on?"

Michael offered to explain while Lucy started packing for them and for the kids.

Later, Lucy and Michael went over to Flora's to see Daraha. She was subdued and kept repeating how sorry she was, but she just couldn't take care of the kids. She was afraid the poacher would come after her, because she could identify him. Michael tried to assure her that the poacher had no reason to feel threatened; he would never be tried for

Pero's death now because it happened too long ago. His explanation hadn't helped. Daraha just dissolved in tears. She kept mumbling something about it being too late for all those people, too. Flora promised Lucy and Michael that she would take care of Daraha and asked them to tell Jane not to worry. She would be here if Jane wanted to call. Lucy and Michael left, wondering how far-reaching the effects of the news of this atrocity would be.

The Vision ...

"We really show that much profit?" Jane was shocked. "I knew we were doing well, but ... what do we do with it?"

"Jane, I've explained to you before. It's important to understand how business works. We have to make money in order to reinvest and grow." Charles had started to recover, Jane noticed. She had liked it better when he was more subdued.

"By 'grow', you mean buying more companies?" Jane was trying to understand.

"Well, that and expanding our portfolio of stocks and bonds. Also, the companies we own have to have investment capital to expand their businesses."

"I don't think...," Jane stopped when she felt Fiona's hand on her arm. She had been doing pretty well, she thought, but Fiona must have observed her energy going into attack formation. They had discussed beforehand ways to keep the meeting productive. Jane knew that meant staying centered and not drawing on anyone else's energy. She refocused and turned to Fiona.

"I think we can take on this discussion in another way," Fiona suggested. "It appears that most of the companies are showing handsome profits, and do have substantial reinvestment funds set up. It is my opinion that an opportunity exists to change the goals of the companies to encourage reinvestment in the community rather than profits for our corporation. I know *I* don't need more money."

"Fiona, we can't just stop making money. It isn't...." Charles stopped when Fiona raised her hand.

"Yes, we can Charles. We can agree on a *reasonable* profit above and beyond our salaries. Then we can use the surplus to correct employee and environmental disparities. Once that is accomplished, we can expand our charitable contributions in the communities where our businesses are located."

"We'll lose all of our business executives! They won't work for a company that's the laughing-stock of Australia." Charles was losing patience. Jane focused on sending him love, hoping it would help. She knew Charles was arguing from his old point of view; it was difficult for him to shift, even though he agreed in principle that a huge price had been paid merely to make a profit.

"Yes, Charles, you are right," Fiona acknowledged. "Some executives will leave. Others will stay, and we will hire new people who have different values to run the companies. We have to do this. It is right, and I firmly believe that it is our responsibility as business and community leaders to shift the way the corporate world does business. I'm not suggesting that we work for nothing. We will concentrate on coming to an agreement on what constitutes a reasonable profit. I just want us to be fair and equitable and moreover, for us to realize that our investment in our communities and the earth will pay much larger dividends than stocks and bonds and money in the bank."

"Charles," Helen joined in "wouldn't you prefer to live in a world of balance and harmony, rather than one filled with strife caused by everyone protecting his own turf and trying to expand it at the expense of others?"

Charles looked desperately at his wife and then at Fiona. "You do realize that what you are suggesting will cause our public stock to be dumped on the market immediately. The price will plummet."

"Yes, Charles, I realize that." Helen was talking to Charles like an equal, which Jane had never heard her mother do before. "I have decided to sell the stock in my private portfolio and buy our corporate stock instead. I've always felt left out. Now I won't be."

Completely surprised and impressed, Jane nodded. "I agree with you, Mother, and I, for once, want to work in the corporation to help make this shift."

"Oh, great!" Charles threw up his hands. "We'll be out of control in no time." He got up and stomped out of the room.

"What did I do now?" Jane groaned. She only wanted to express her enthusiasm. She hadn't meant to upset Charles.

"Don't worry, Jane," Helen comforted her, "Charles is just confused right now. His entire world has turned upside-down overnight, and he no longer knows what to do. It will take a while. Just try to keep being gentle and loving with him. That's is all we can do."

Mother's right, Jane thought. It's all we can do. He will have to come to terms with this situation in his own way. Jane continued to be amazed with the way Fiona had been coping with the news of Harold's suicide. She was concerned about Fiona not dealing with her feelings and asked Fiona about it as delicately as she could.

Fiona opened up to her, "Jane, somewhere deep inside, I must have always known. I have been preparing for this

day for a long time. All my self-studying, and the understanding I've gained as I have become more spiritually
conscious, has prepared me to take action at the right time.
Now is that time and I *know* I am being guided. My role, my
purpose, is to help change the direction that business is
taking. I happen to be in the unique position to do just that.
I'm extremely thankful to be here now and to have this
opportunity." Fiona had a serene and peaceful air about her.

Jane reached over and squeezed Fiona's hand. She
glanced at the clock. It was nearly time for Lucy and
Michael to arrive. This was going to be an exciting meeting.
Finally, it seemed there would be an opportunity to put their
shared beliefs into practice. Jane, Lucy and Michael had
had so many discussions about how they would like to
change the way companies affected the environment. Now,
they could do it. She hoped Lucy and Michael were as
revved up about it as she was. The secretary buzzed the
inner office. Lucy and Michael just arrived.

The Exposé …

The Sunday Australian exposé on "the Big Reef
Refinery massacre" as it was being called, created the anticipated havoc. Gary London appeared on the evening news
denying he knew anything whatsoever about the incident.
Charles was furious. Luckily, his own reaction had already
been printed, thanks to Peg Wild. Actually, Miss Wild
portrayed Charles rather sympathetically in her article. She
blamed the poacher and Harold entirely for the ugly
incident, not once suggesting that Charles had any
knowledge of the murders. Still, Lawton-Starr lawyers and
public relations staff had their hands full. Ultimately, they
did a good job redirecting the public's attention toward all

the changes occurring in the corporation. They emphasized how new priorities were being instituted as a direct reaction to the horrific news.

Fiona was particularly effective when interviewed on television. Her personal anguish over the horror of the incident was accepted as genuine. She spoke of her changing role in the corporation and underlined the importance of business taking an active part to create positive change in society. She acknowledged that her vision would alter the economic structure of Australia if it was adopted by a majority of companies in the country. Her statement made Fiona the talk of financial news programs all over the western world. *Of course, the reaction was one of levity.* But Fiona didn't mind. The concept was introduced into the minds of people as a possibility; that alone was worth any amount of criticism or jokes.

Within the week, Fiona was interviewed on several women's talk shows, where the hosts took her seriously. Reactions from the Aboriginal press and Aborigines who were surveyed, were less than optimistic. Occasionally, though, a voice rang out reminding people to wait and see the results of the changes that were being made.

Toward the end of the week, Charles, Fiona and Michael began their mission to visit each company owned by the corporation, in order to explain the new corporate priorities to all employees before the changes were instituted. They hoped to avert any unrest. The changes were drastic enough that, if they weren't supported by management, poor communication could cause workers to be afraid of losing their jobs. Fiona wanted to deflect such worries before they started.

Meanwhile, Jane and Lucy flew back up north to Wainton to tie up loose ends. Both of them planned to move down to the city to be near corporate headquarters, but the transition would take some time. Neither talked much during the long flight since they were tired and needed time to think.

Lucy wanted to hire a technical manager for their business. She had already arranged for two interviews, and since there were several qualified Ph.D.'s on the market, she and Michael were confident they would find someone suitable. Additionally, the business manager they had hired last year was working out well, and would be helpful in getting the new technical manager up to speed. Lucy was trying to decide whether to lease their house or just close it up and use it for holidays or when they came to town to visit the company. Her major concern, however, was the children. She wanted to make the transition as easy as possible for them. They were used to being cared for by Daraha and her mother, now they would be in daycare. When Fiona heard Michael and Lucy discussing their concerns about their children, she put 'daycare for employee's children' on her priority list. The new corporate policy said that any company that could not offer in-house daycare, would contract with an outside care facility. Several secretaries at corporate headquarters who had children were ecstatic. One even volunteered to find a suitable daycare nearby.

Jane had other concerns. There would be lots of upheaval in Wainton. The sugar refinery was the town's largest employer and a scandal like this was sure to cause havoc. She was worried about Daraha. Jane hadn't heard back from her all week, even though Jane had left messages at Flora's twice. Surely, Daraha had regained control of her fear of the poacher by now. And then there was Bob. She had to make their breakup official. Everything had happened so fast, that she had only seen him briefly the morning after their fight, when he was packing some clothes to stay at his mate's apartment. She supposed he knew everything that had happened. He may even have moved already back into the house they shared. That could complicate things, she predicted. After all it would be Bob's house now. Well, she could always stay at Lucy's, if necessary.

Jane had another concern. She didn't know what her role would be in the reorganized corporation. She knew she wanted to be involved, and she supposed she would help Fiona, but she sensed there was another role for her, one that hadn't been identified yet. Jane thought, that perhaps, spending some time with Flora in the rainforest would help her shed some light on the matter.

At the Wainton airport, Jane and Lucy were surprised when reporters surrounded them, firing loud and overlapping questions at them. Jane and Lucy stopped; Jane held up her hand. "Please, one at a time. We will try to answer a few questions."

"What do you think about the strike?"

"Has your father been questioned by the police yet?"

"What is your family going to do to make up for the murders here in Wainton?"

Jane was startled by the force with which the questions were being asked. Frightened she turned to confer with Lucy, but her friend had disappeared. As the reporters pressed in closer to her, Jane backed away. She wanted to flee. A moment later, Lucy reappeared with some security guards, who took over by surrounding Jane and Lucy and escorting them quickly through a private door and out of sight of the reporters.

"Whew! That was horrible. What were they talking about?" Jane asked one of the security guards.

"All the Aboriginal workers at the sugar refinery stayed home on Monday, after they heard the news. They haven't been to work all week; this morning the entire plant was shut down by court order. I'm surprised you didn't hear about it."

Jane grimaced. The national news had reported some workers did not show up on Monday at the Wainton refinery, but she hadn't realized it was this bad. She and Lucy must have left for the airport before the news broke about the court order. She had better get PR on the phone as soon as possible. She knew she couldn't make a statement until she had their input, and she didn't want to make any mistakes. It crossed her mind that Charles might be taken in for questioning.

Lucy had made arrangements for her mother, Marilyn to pick up the two travelers at the airport. Marilyn arrived just in time and they got away only seconds before the reporters discovered their whereabouts. "This is ridiculous," Lucy commented. "I don't see how we're going to get anything done."

"I think you both should stay at my place until things quiet down. You can work from there," Marilyn was trying to be helpful.

"That's probably best for Lucy. Then she can be with the kids, but I think I shall just go home."

"Jane, don't be ridiculous," Lucy admonished her, "you can't go there. The reporters know exactly where you live. They'll be camping out on your doorstep. Why don't we both go to Mom's and make some phone calls?"

"Okay," Jane agreed, resignedly.

Two hours later, Bob drove up to Marilyn's house in Jane's Land Rover. "Hello, there!" He greeted everyone as he walked in. "You have been having quite the adventure, I guess. Well, so has everyone in this town. Let me tell you! It's easy for me to leave the store now, because there aren't any customers. Everyone is afraid of what is going to happen to the economy if the sugar refinery shuts down for good." He glanced around like a wounded but brave animal.

"Bob, hello … wow … I didn't even think about the refinery shutting down. That is really drastic," Jane was concerned.

"That is typical, Jane, you never think."

"Please, let's not argue," Jane requested, "it's not worth it. Thank you very much for bringing my car and some of my things. Do you have time to chat for a while, before I drop you back at work?" Jane knew it was best if they made their breakup official as soon as possible.

"No, not really. I should get back. I have to let some of the employees go home early so I can just keep the store open with minimum staff. We can talk on the way." Bob didn't want to postpone the inevitable any more than she did.

"All right, we'll go now." Jane picked up her purse and walked out the door he held open. Bob started to go around to the driver's side, then, realized he wouldn't be driving her car anymore. He turned, walked back, handed her the keys and got in the passenger side.

Jane noted the gesture, got in and backed out of the drive. She drove down the road until she saw a small sidetrack and turned in. Stopping the car, she turned to Bob with a lump in her throat. "I'm sorry, Bob. I never thought it would turn out like this. I honestly wanted to be happy with you. But it's been such a long time since we were happy together." She reached in her purse and took out the diamond he had given her twice. "It is a beautiful ring just like I *thought* we were beautiful together once, but," she paused a moment, "I never *think*. Right?" She tried to smile wittily as she handed him the ring; instead, tears started rolling down her cheeks.

Chapter Ten

The Reaction

⑥　　⑥　　⑥

After Jane dropped Bob off and collected herself, she headed to Michael and Lucy's office. Reporters were lingering around the front door, so Jane drove on and doubled back down the alley where she parked. She rummaged around in the back seat and found her old hat, pulled it on low over her face, walked to the back door and slipped in the building unnoticed. Lucy had alerted Barb, the office manager, to have two cell phones ready for Jane. They figured it was better to stay in constant touch with so much going on.

One mission accomplished, Jane drove out to Lucy's house. There was a strange car in the driveway – probably a reporter – so Jane didn't stop. Jane found it hard to believe that there were so many reporters around. She hoped they would get bored and go home or that some other big scandal would break and they would all be reassigned. Fat chance! She called Lucy to warn her about the reporter and to tell her that she was on her way to Flora's.

No one was home at Flora's which was strange, because there were so many grandchildren who usually hung out there. Jane decided to try Daraha's. She didn't really think they'd be there, since Daraha was so afraid the poacher would find her, but she didn't know where else to look, except the Aboriginal Centre. As she drove up to the small cement house, she saw a new Toyota parked beside Flora's old white car. She wondered who else was there and hoped it wasn't a reporter. She decided to risk it anyway. It was worth it to see Daraha.

A young light-skinned Aborigine with unruly long hair pulled back into a single braid answered the door. "Yo! Help you?" His tone was cold and flat.

"I'm looking for Daraha and Flora, please."

Daraha came rushing to the door past the man and gave Jane a big hug. "Oh, Jane! Come in, come in. See who's here. Bet you don't know them. So good to see you here."

Jane was thrown off. Daraha was seldom this demonstrative. She allowed herself to be pulled into the bare living room. Inside were Flora, the man who had answered the door, and an attractive Aboriginal woman about Jane's age, perhaps a little older. The woman was well dressed in a linen pantsuit and wore her hair tightly pulled back in a bun. Jane noticed the man and woman bore a slight resemblance to each other. No one spoke. Jane realized they were waiting to see if she recognized them.

"I'm afraid I am at a disad...." Jane started speaking, then stopped. It couldn't be she thought, not both of them at the same time! Tears welled up in her eyes and she swallowed hard. She felt her face flushing. "Are you...?" She was afraid to say it.

"Yes, yes, yes!" Daraha was nearly jumping up and down. "All my children come home at same time."

Jane's cautious expression dissolved into a warm, embracing smile. "Oh, I am so glad! Our newspaper interview ... is that how you found Daraha?"

"Least you don't call her Mum!" Possum remarked with disgust, as he went toward the door. "Think I'll walk down for lemonade. Want to go Peg?"

"Peg?" Jane said nearly involuntarily. She was shocked. It couldn't be. But she recalled Charles describing Peg Wild, and Oonta certainly fit the description.

"Yes, I'm Peg Wild. I'm the one who exposed your family secret." Peg stood up as if to go out with Possum.

"And you did a fine job, too. Thank you." Jane responded immediately with an outstretched hand.

Peg tilted her head back and didn't offer her hand in return. She raised an eyebrow and inquired, "You aren't angry with me?"

"No! Why should I be? Thanks to you, now the truth is out and we have a marvelous opportunity to make some much-needed changes in our corporation, which, I hope, will bring about a lot more change in the business world, and in our entire culture." Jane beamed with enthusiasm.

"A Pollyanna!" Peg retorted, her voice laced with sarcasm. "How sweet. Good luck to you. Now, I think I will accompany my brother. If you will excuse me. It has been a pleasure meeting you."

Peg nodded in mock politeness at Jane and started for the door.

"Oonta! That's not nice." Daraha stepped in front of Peg. "Jane's wonderful to me and I hope you all be close, like when you little."

"Sorry, Mom. It is hard enough just trying to figure out how I feel finding out you are alive and still living here. There is no way I'm going to take to heart a 'sister' who caused all our misery." With that Peg pushed out the door with Possum right behind her.

Jane, in shock, sat down on the threadbare sofa. Why was it always her fault? She looked at her hands, then up at Daraha who just stood there, her eyes fixed on the door.

"I'm so sorry, Daraha. I would never have come if I'd known. I just wanted to see you. I'd better go. If they see me leave, they will come back." Jane stood up and started for the door.

Flora put out her hand and stopped her. "Jane, this not your fault. Our young people are always angry when they come home, if they come. Be patient, perhaps they'll work through it."

"No, Flora. I have caused so much pain for Daraha. It really is entirely my fault and I am so sorry. I don't know what to do." Jane could feel the tears coming, and she wanted to get out of there and hide.

"Please, Jane. Don't go. It's not your fault. I knew Possum mad. But thought Oonta okay. Thought she just angry at poacher and Harold Starr. She didn't say any other thing about your family."

Jane started crying openly. Her life had caused so much pain. How could she ever make it up to this wonderful woman? The only thing she could do was leave so Daraha's own children would come back to her. She hugged Daraha and moved toward the door.

Daraha tried to hold her back, but Flora laid her hand on Daraha saying softly, "Let her go for now. I'll talk with her tomorrow."

Jane drove slowly back to Marilyn's. She felt totally lost, like she didn't have a friend in the world. When she walked into the kitchen and saw Lucy, she collapsed, releasing the sadness she was holding back. It was quite a while before Lucy was able to get the story out of her.

Jane woke up curled up tight in a ball again. She stretched and the old pain shot through her hip. She gasped. It was back! She had been doing so well; why now? Jane had so much to do; now she wouldn't be able to tackle any of it. She leaned back against the headboard and thought of Daraha and the scene with Possum and Peg. It was all her fault. Now she wouldn't be able to be with Daraha anymore, since her presence might keep that dear woman from having a close relationship with her real children. Jane moaned. She was no-one's real child. She felt incredibly lonely. Even Bob was gone now. What was she going to do?

Jane was lying there, thinking how fate had handed her such a raw deal, when Lucy burst into the room. "They found the bodies! Come watch the telly."

"I can't. I can't get up. It's my hip!" Jane was talking in her weepy voice.

Lucy looked at her. "I'm sorry you don't feel so well. I'll bring you a coffee." She left the room. Sometimes, Jane's "poor-little-me" attitude was slightly overdone, to say the least. Lucy had never enjoyed being around Jane when she was feeling sorry for herself. She carried the coffee back in the room where she found Jane still lying in her bed whimpering.

"Jane, I know you are going through a lot right now," Lucy tried to be understanding, "but I thought you told me you were learning how to increase your energy field, so your hip wouldn't hurt anymore. Here's your coffee. I'm going to watch the news." Lucy put the coffee down on a table beside Jane, and left.

Jane's eyes followed Lucy out. Her friend just didn't understand that Jane couldn't get her energy field to increase; she'd been trying. She needed someone to help her. Lucy had never had to go through anything like this. Her mother had always been there for her. Really, Lucy was her friend, she should be more sympathetic.

The phone rang and Lucy came back in shortly. "It's for you. It's Flora."

"Please tell her I'm in too much pain to get up and come now. I'll try to call her later."

Lucy rolled up her eyes as she turned to go back to the phone. She returned a few minutes later. "They are going to walk to the sugar refinery. Flora wanted you to know what was happening and that she wouldn't be coming around today, like she told you yesterday."

Jane raised up on one elbow, wincing as she did. "Who is walking there? From where?"

"All the Aboriginals are gathering at the Aboriginal Centre and walking together to the refinery for a ceremony. They are starting at ten this morning. They are going to walk right through the middle of Wainton."

Jane forced herself into a sitting position. "I think we'd better call headquarters. Have you talked to Michael this morning?"

"Yes, he called earlier. They have decided to fly back to headquarters before going out again."

"Good, then they can all decide what to do. Give me ten minutes. I will try to get up."

The Walk ...

Jane, Lucy, Marilyn and the children waited downtown, standing on the corner in front of the music store where Jane had once bought the CD with a song about the sugar refinery. How appropriate it would be, Jane thought, if the store would play that song over its speaker system now ... but all was silent. The streets were lined with so many white people standing in respect as the local Aborigines walked through town. There had been some hecklers, as always, but the majority had stared them down. Jane's body was tense. She stood leaning against a lightpost and on her cane. She was irritated that she was having so much pain. Try as she might, she could not get it to ease up. Maybe when Fiona arrived later in the day, she would be able to help.

"There they are!" Lucy pointed down the street. Jane looked and saw Daraha and Flora. Right behind them were their families. There were lots of adults and children behind Flora and only two with Daraha. But, they were there. Jane had wondered if Peg would walk. She knew Possum would. But Jane didn't know what to think about Peg.

Flora spotted Jane, and headed straight for her. She stopped directly in front of her and said pointedly, "I see you have decided for your hip to hurt again. I had hoped you were past that." She turned briskly and rejoined the group. Daraha, who had also walked over, reached out and touched Jane's hand on the cane, smiled lovingly. Then she turned and followed Flora.

Tears of shame and sorrow streaked down Jane's cheeks. She watched as both families walked, each person staring at her as they passed. She kept her eyes riveted on the sea of black faces as they slowly moved through the street: old and young, babies on their mothers' backs, fathers carrying young children, teens walking slowly to assist the elder family members. It was a long walk that would probably take all day as the refinery was twenty miles south of Wainton. The day was uncomfortably hot already. Only a few of the Aborigines were carrying water. Jane hoped they would be okay.

Suddenly, a cluster of reporters surged through the crowd making a beeline for Jane and Lucy. Quickly, Marilyn handed Katrina to Lucy, stepped in front of Jane who winced slightly, and followed her friend into the music store, where they quietly slipped out the back door and made for the car. As soon as Marilyn joined them, they drove off hurriedly.

Fiona and Michael flew in later that afternoon. Since the airport was south of town on the same road as the refinery, and the road was closed until the procession passed, Michael and Fiona walked out to the highway and watched. When Michael and Fiona finally arrived at Marilyn's house, they found everyone glued to the TV. The first of the Aborigines had arrived at Big Reef Refinery and found the gates locked and armed guards and dogs stationed behind the fence. Reporters were trying to contact management of Big Reef to get a statement. The Aboriginal people simply sat down, in front of the entrance, right on the road, which effectively blocked all traffic on the coastal highway. Traffic had been at a standstill all day due to the procession, but the police had been helpful, setting up necessary road blocks and arranging the few detours that were possible.The media had cooperated too, thus far. Announcements were made on radio and TV asking travelers to wait until evening when the roads would be opened again. Now it was clear that the main highway couldn't be reopened until the Aboriginals moved.

Police using bullhorns ordered everyone to move to the sides of the roadway, but there was no place for the people to go. One side of the highway was refinery property with a high wire fence stretching for nearly a mile along the road. The other side was a steep, rocky cliff overlooking the beach, which was presently underwater because the tide was in. The waves were knocking roughly over the rocks. Since there was nowhere to go except onto the sharp rocks, the Aborigines stayed in the middle of the road. A group of elders sat in a circle directly in front of the gate. TV cameras scanned their faces regularly and reporters tried to set up microphones to hear what the elders were saying, but apparently no one was talking.

A television camera panned across Flora sitting in the circle of elders. Jane thought she saw Daraha's face directly behind her. The television coverage was national now, the Premier of Queensland was flying into Wainton. News and medical helicopters were hovering overhead in anticipation of something unfolding. Jane was beginning to panic. She couldn't sit still, but her hip hurt so much she couldn't walk around either. Her breathing was shallow and she realized she was sweating despite the air conditioning. Fiona came over and sat down on the sofa beside her.

"Jane, your energy field is extremely depleted," she said softly. "Would you like for me to help you into the other room, away from the television, so you can see if you can get back into balance?"

Jane struggled to tear her eyes away from the telly. She knew she would feel better if she did as Fiona suggested, but she didn't want to. She felt she should stay here by the TV. It was as close as she could get to Daraha, and she felt a need to be there for her. Fiona touched her arm again and Jane finally nodded, reaching for her cane.

Once they were alone, Jane refocused and followed Fiona's voice as she went through the breathing technique. Soon she felt a sense of lightness about her, as though her entire being had expanded. Once she reached this level, she relaxed. She could think more clearly. After a few minutes, Jane commented to Fiona, "I haven't been this low for a long time."

"That's true, but you have been through a lot during the last few days. Do you want to talk about it?"

"I just keep thinking that my whole life has been a lie, that I have to do something to make up to Daraha and all the Aboriginal people for who I am and all the pain I have caused."

The corners of Fiona's mouth twitched as if she were beginning to smile and thought better of it. "That is quite a responsibility you have heaped on yourself. Do you think I am responsible also?"

"Oh, no! You have always tried to help. You didn't know what Uncle Harold had done. Apparently, he didn't either until it was too late. I just feel that my life somehow is so intertwined in this mess that it has to be my fault. Pero wouldn't have been killed if I hadn't been there, and then Uncle Harold wouldn't have known that awful poacher either, and none of this would have happened."

Fiona just shook her head and decided to remind Jane of a new way of thinking. "Jane, remember last week when we were determining what our corporation would do? We decided to focus on the *present* and how our actions could shift the future. We cannot change the past, or those who wish to stay in the past, but we can be responsible for our own actions in the present and make choices that will provide opportunities for change in the future. This was our unanimous choice as a family unit and as a corporation.

Think about Charles, when he has difficulty remembering this choice and he speaks from a past position. Is this similar to you and your thoughts about Pero and the Aboriginals?"

"I don't think so, Aunt Fiona. But I don't know. I'll think about it, though. I seem to be pretty confused. But, really, I'm not like Charles, am I?" Jane muddled.

"We are all alike in many ways, Jane. Just remember that you are making the choices for your own life."

Michael stuck his head in the door, "The premier is going to hold a news conference in half an hour. There are reports that he is bringing in the police in riot gear to remove the Aboriginal people from state and private properties and force them to go back home."

"Oh, my God!" Jane sprung up, cringing as she grabbed for her cane. "He can't do that, he just can't! People will get hurt. We have to do something!" She headed toward the family room to see the news with Fiona and Michael following right behind.

A reporter in the city was interviewing Reverend Paul Rivers, the distinguished minister from the Uniting Church, whose stellar career began with this work with the Aborigines on missions in the outback. He had become well known for his books on Aboriginal spirituality. His understanding of Aboriginal culture had enabled him to mediate several times between the Euro-Australians and the Aboriginals. Also, he had been influential in negotiating for Aboriginal land rights.

He began his effort now to foster communication: "I'm sure all the Aboriginal people want to do is have a ceremony to release the spirits of the dead family. It has been my experience, from my work in missions in the outback, that even large gatherings such as this are nearly always for a ceremony. If you ask me, they should be allowed to have their ceremony and then they will go home on their own."

"Would you be willing to go to Wainton to mediate?" The reporter asked.

"Certainly," the reverend responded. "It would be highly preferable to using police action. I'm offering my assistance to the premier." With that, the reporter broke away, saying the premier's limousine was nearing the refinery.

Television coverage shifted back to the Big Reef Refinery. Cameras scanned the Aboriginal people as they made way for the motorcycle police and the limousine. The limousine approached the front gates of the refinery, then came to a halt, unable to go any farther without hitting the circle of unmoving Aboriginal elders. After a long pause a door of the limousine door opened, and the premier climbed out, along with Gary London, the owner of Big Reef Refinery. They were flanked by bodyguards and trailed by reporters as they walked carefully around the elders to stand directly in front of the gates, where a microphone and speakers had been set up.

London spoke a few brief words, offering his condolences to the Aborigines and again denying any knowledge of the tragedy. He also stated that no one except official employees of Big Reef Refinery were allowed inside the gates or on the property in any location. The premier stepped forward, extending his sympathies and promising that the person or persons who had committed this atrocity would be prosecuted to the full extent of the law. He then stated that he could not allow the highway to remain closed, or for private property to be threatened, and he requested that the Aboriginal people return to their homes.

The circle of elders did not move or respond in any way to the premier's statement. As he and London returned to the limousine, reporters bombarded them with many questions that the premier declined to answer. When they left, speculating reporters suggested riot squad police teams soon would arrive to clear the area.

As she watched the events on the television, Jane realized that the Aborigines were not going to leave and that they had neither food nor water. She voiced her concern to Fiona, who looked at Jane with wide eyes.

"Of course! I've been sitting here trying to come up with an appropriate way to show my concern and support for the Aboriginal people – and this is it." Quickly, Fiona reached into her purse and pulled out her cell phone and started dialing as she walked out of the room.

Michael turned to Lucy and said, "You call the restaurants and ask for donations. I'll start calling the grocery stores. We'll need bottled water, too."

Fiona, meanwhile, walked back in, saying, "Charles agrees. He is so mad at Gary London, he'd probably risk the entire business to see London forced to acknowledge his role in all this. Charles and Helen are going to fly up on the corporate jet with Reverend Paul Rivers. They saw him interviewed on the telly and decided to ask him if he would like to join our efforts. Our jobs are to get the water and food organized and to have transportation at the airport in two hours. Jane, Charles specifically said that if we're going to take a stand, we're all going to do it together."

They made it with only moments to spare. It had been easy to get donations as everyone they approached had donated something. A bakery offered one of its delivery trucks, plus bread and several hundred freshly-baked meat pies. Bottled water and lemonades had also been donated.

Several restaurants and other businesses promised to help with more food for the following day if needed. Jane was gratified by the community's response. It was as though something had awakened in the hearts of the white people of Wainton as they watched their black neighbors move slowly through the streets of their town.

Helen hugged Jane as she walked into the airport. Charles was talking to Fiona and the minister and, as usual, just nodded to her on his way by. Oh well, thought Jane, at least we are on the same side now. When they climbed into the van, Jane found herself sitting next to Reverend Rivers.

"I was very happy to hear your statement on the news and am so glad you decided to join us in our effort to show support for these people," Jane began politely.

"I was delighted when Charles called. I have often wanted to contact your family, and I must confess my regret that I never took the time before. You see, I'm related to your birth father, Rod Rivers. He was my nephew."

Jane was too shocked to speak and Fiona, who had overheard the conversation, intervened. "Really, Reverend, I never related the surnames. We always wondered whether Rod had any family, but when no one came forward even with all the publicity that surrounded Jane being found in the rainforest, we assumed there were no living relatives."

The reverend looked slightly embarrassed. "There were reasons why I didn't come forward. I was going to make myself known but then there was the kidnapping trial. I just couldn't then." Everyone in the van had tuned in by now. The reverend looked around. He had been introduced to everyone and knew that only family was present; and Lucy and Michael were close family friends. He paused for a moment and then confided to them.

"Everyone has secrets and I am no exception. The one secret of my adult life has propelled me into the role I now assume regularly, of being a vocal supporter of Aboriginal rights. You see, when I was a young man, I was assigned to an Aboriginal mission in the outback. I had no wife and I was very lonely. There was a wonderful young Aboriginal woman, who was assigned to clean my rooms and cook for me. She was always very kind to me. After a while we became lovers and she bore my child. We kept the secret, and as far as I know she never told anyone. I saw to it that she always had work and was treated fairly by her employees. She worked mainly on sheep stations and eventually she married. Her husband didn't live long, though. He worked in the asbestos mines and smoked, too. She came to see me after he died and told me that our daughter had married. Narana needed work again, so I sent her to work for my nephew, Rod, who had recently married and was trying to establish a sheep station some distance away from the mission where I was working.

"I was very shocked when I learned of Rod and Mary's deaths. I assumed Narana had perished from the bad water also, since I never heard from her again. Later, when she was put on trial, I was too embarrassed to come forward. To be honest, I was afraid I would lose my standing in the church," Reverend Rivers drew in a sharp breath.

"This is the first time I've told anyone. But when Charles contacted me today, I decided I must tell you all the truth. Your family's response last week was the most courageous acknowledgment of the past that I have heard. And when I was given the opportunity to join your move toward a better future, I realized it was God telling me that now is the time for all of us to share the pain of our past, hope for healing, and pray for love and acceptance of each other in the future."

Everyone was silent when he finished. Jane felt an overpowering love toward the reverend who was sitting next to her. This man was responsible for her relationship to Narana. He was Daraha's father and he was also her great uncle. That meant that she was related to Daraha. She tried to say something but no words came. Fiona reached over and took her hand. A thoughtful silence had settled over the passengers in the car. When they reached the edge of the Aboriginal gathering, the reverend quietly suggested they pray.

A few minutes later a policeman stopped the van and asked what they were doing there. Satisfied with Michael's explanation, the officer waved them on, the delivery truck following closely behind. Next, Possum, who recognized Jane through the window, stopped them. "What you doing here?" he asked accusingly.

"Possum, please. We've brought food for your people. Could you take us to Flora and Daraha?"

Possum backed away from the van, but nodded, "I think it better that you walk. The truck and van will be fine here."

They all disembarked and walked behind Possum to the circle of elders. When they reached the elders, Fiona, assuming her role as the family elder, stepped forward.

"We have come to express our sorrow for the part our family played in this tragedy. We do not expect your forgiveness, only that you consider accepting our offer of support for your endeavors here. We have brought food and water for your people, and will do so each day you are here. Also, we have brought the Reverend Paul Rivers, who has come to offer his assistance to you in any way you find acceptable. Thank you for listening to me." Fiona stepped back. Reporters surrounded her with questions, but Michael and Possum intercepted them and asked them to stand back.

The elders looked around at each other, then one at a time they nodded. The oldest man in the group spoke. "We accept your offer. You may give food to our people. We will talk to the reverend." The council remained seated, but other Aboriginals closest to them got up. One of the men approached Michael and offered to help distribute the food.

Daraha got up and went to Jane and put out her hands. "You have brought my father."

"Yes, he told us," Jane replied with wonder. "You already knew?"

"Yes, Narana said just before she die. I never met him before. You introduce me."

Jane gestured across the circle to the reverend, who nodded quizzically, until the sight of Daraha hit him. He quickly excused himself from the reporter he was talking to and walked around the elders to Jane and Daraha.

"Hello, my daughter," he offered her a gentle smile.

"Hello, Father," Daraha had tears in her eyes. "I was angry at you for many years, but I know your work is important. Understand now, if you come an' take care of me when little, you never do great things in your church and for my people. Narana tol' me to be proud. Finally," Daraha took a deep breath and let out a long sigh, "proud."

"Thank you, Daraha, my daughter. May I have your permission to announce our relationship to the world?"

"Oh, not now. Please, want time to tell my children." Daraha was suddenly afraid, especially of what Peg would do or say, when she found out who her grandfather was. "And you have important things to do here."

"Yes, of course. I will wait until you're ready. You're right, I must attend to business." The reverend nodded respectfully at Daraha and Jane and turned and went to join the news conference that Fiona and Charles were holding.

The Result ...

The sit-down progressed to its third day. The premier had not yet used force to remove the Aboriginal people, although pressure from the business interests was mounting. On the other hand, public sentiment remained strongly supportive of the Aborigines. The incident had captured the attention of the international press and had even made an appearance on the network evening news in the United States. Food and money gifts were pouring in from all over the world. The council of elders asked Reverend Rivers to set up a fund to receive the monies for the Aboriginal community. At least one member of Jane's family remained with the Aboriginal people at all times, along with Reverend Paul, who refused to leave at all. They hoped their presence would help deter police action, and the sad reality was that it probably had.

Just as things were about to collide, the State Department of Natural Resources announced that they had captured the poacher. One of the poacher's sons had tipped off the police as to his possible whereabouts because he was angry that his father hadn't paid his sons' poaching fines, and left them in jail. The front page of the newspaper splashed a picture of the poacher escorted into the courthouse wearing one of the strange cabbage palm hats that he obviously made himself. The media began speculating wildly on what would happen next. The Aboriginal people were growing restless. Some felt compelled to talk to reporters for the first time.

They demanded that the white establishment punish the poacher for his atrocities immediately.

Before long, the poacher's lawyer released a statement that he had given to the police in an effort to obtain leniency. The poacher claimed that Gary London, the present owner of the refinery, had actually been the individual who ordered the killings. Harold Starr had only arranged the meeting between the poacher and London. Starr had been completely unaware of the killings until the poacher attempted to blackmail him later.

The moment this news was released, Reverend Rivers appeared on television calling for the government to seize the refinery and open the gates to the Aboriginal people. He personally guaranteed that no damage would be done to the property. After a few hours' delay, the gates were opened and the Aboriginal people were allowed in. No guards, police or reporters accompanied them, as they had requested to hold their ceremony in private.

The next day, when the Aboriginal people began leaving the refinery to return home, buses were sent from Wainton to offer them a ride home. Although reporters were still around trying to stir up controversy, a sense of peace prevailed among those who had been directly affected by the revelation of the tragedy and its aftermath.

Following the announcement of London's arrest for his role in the massacre, Charles and Fiona were on the phone with corporate lawyers negotiating the purchase of the refinery. The deal was made in less than twenty-four hours. It was unique in the history of Australia: All the employees, ninety percent of whom were Aboriginal, were given one-third of the ownership. The sugar cane farmers who contracted exclusively with the refinery and agreed to the new environmental practices were offered stock options,

which would total one-third of the ownership if all were
purchased. The Lawton-Starr Corporation held the
remaining one-third. Additionally, the land surrounding the
refinery would be deeded to the Aboriginal community.
London's profits from the sale of the refinery would be
garnished to pay for the environmental cleanup. Big Reef
Refinery reopened for business the following Monday.

The Heritage ...

"Oonta, Possum. Something need talk about." Daraha
ran her hands along the edge of the table in front of her.

"I'm Peg, Mom. Please!"

"Yes, Peg. Try, but just don't want you lose heritage."

"The white world is my heritage, too, isn't it?" Peg
snapped.

"Well, I'm Possum. I didn't like being called Bill."
Possum joined in from across the room, where he was
bending down and tying his shoes. "What do you need to
talk about, Mum? Gotta go meet my mate."

"I've been worry 'bout telling you, all during sit-
down." Daraha twisted the hem of her apron around her
fingers.

"Not about Jane, is it? I had about all can take of her
anyway, even if her family brought food and everything."
Possum sounded irritated.

"No, no. I do wish you give her chance, though. She
so confused, just like you two." Daraha started feeling that
perhaps it wasn't the right time to tell them more. Too much
had happened.

"Come on Mom. Out with it." Peg was getting
annoyed by all the family caring and closeness; it scared
her, actually.

Daraha sighed. "Okay.. I want to tell you who your grandfather. He asked me if he could announce that he my father but said, 'No, tell my children first."

"On with it. We haven't got all day and it's not going to make a piddling bit of difference to me. I've got to go back to Sydney soon. My boss has been calling me." Peg knew if she had to listen to one more confession, she would scream.

"Narana told me before she passed on. Very angry at first, because thought if he help us, maybe no one take you away. Later, see that if he had tol' and come help us, he can't do many important things he did. Now, he wants to tell truth."

"So he wants to acknowledge us? Maybe we don't want to be acknowledged!" Peg threw out.

"Yeah," Possum interjected. "It makes no bloody difference in my life."

"I think it will. He Reverend Paul Rivers." Daraha watched their faces closely as she said his name. Peg's face froze; not even one muscle moved. Possum's reaction was immediate. His face contorted violently. He stood up, knocked a chair over with the side of his arm, and strode toward the door.

"That fucking bastard!" Possum voice was loud and off key. "He has no right to speak for Aborigines. He's bad like that businessman who owned refinery." Possum stopped at the door. "Tell him stay away from me." And Possum tore out the house.

Daraha sat staring at her hands. She had known it was going to be awful. She didn't want to lose her kids; she had just gotten them back, but she felt telling them and the world, was important, too. Flora said healing had to start in your own house and after all she'd been through in her life, she wanted her house finally healed.

"Mom," Peg interrupted Daraha's train of thought. "Call him and tell him I want to be the one to write his story. Maybe that will help me understand. Right now, I feel angry and hurt, but I worked hard as an objective reporter to tell both sides of a story. Usually I understand quicker and a lot better if I am the reporter."

"Oo…, I mean Peg, thank you. I thought you did good job about this refinery business. You real fair." Daraha peered into her daughter's face and silently prayed. "Will talk to him. Would you talk with Flora, too?"

"Why is that relevant?" Peg challenged

"She sees big picture on things better. And I believe that's important. Just talk to her before you write article. Okay?"

"Sure, Mom. I promise. Well, I need to go back to Sydney tomorrow. Do you want to do something special today?"

"Walk in rainforest with me?" Daraha asked hopefully. Peg nodded. That afternoon, mother and daughter walked down the track into the deep canopy of another world, just as they had twenty years before.

Chapter Eleven

The Memory

⑥　　⑥　　⑥

"Jane, we are going to a special place today," Flora announced when Jane got out of her car and walked over to her. "This old rainforest has many secrets. I saw in a dream last night that it is important to reveal this one to you."

A flock of cockatoos screeched as they flew out of a nearby tree. Jane looked up at them disturbed by the noise. A secret. Jane wondered if she was up to this. She had had about all the secrets she could take lately. Out of nowhere, she felt like crying. Flora touched her hand as the tears started down Jane's cheeks.

"I'm sorry, Flora. I know you don't like it when I feel sorry for myself, but my hip hurts so bad. Everything feels wrong to me, even though I know it's all right. I know everything has turned out for the best. Daraha has her children back and her father. My family owns the sugar refinery again and is changing it for the better. If everything is so positive, why do I feel so bad?" Jane choked back a sob.

Flora just took Jane's hand and pulled her along. "Come on now. Let's go find the secret."

They picked their way down a narrow track into the rainforest. It was dark; the canopy was very thick. Flora cautioned Jane to watch where she put her feet as the track was slippery. Birds sang out occasionally and insects buzzed around Jane's head. Slowly, she stopped sniffling, concentrated on breathing deeply, and just being in the moment. She felt better for a while, but then, she realized she was wanted to cry again. She didn't understand why she felt so sad. Then she recognized the smell.

"Flora, there is honeysuckle here."

"Yes, my child. Warrah is growing on the tops of the trees. Look up."

"The Aboriginal name for honeysuckle is 'warrah'?" Jane asked peering up into the canopy.

"That's right," Flora responded. Then she continued in a lower tone of voice. "My dream showed you sitting under a warrah vine crying. As we walk, you might try concentrating on the smell of the warrah. Try to remember every time you have ever smelled it."

"That's easy," Jane replied. "I cried, every time I smelled it." Jane started recounting all the times when she was a young teenager and was made fun of for crying when she was around honeysuckle. After she finished, Flora stopped walking and smiled at her.

"Now, Jane, take a deep breath. Smell the warrah and try to remember the last time you were here."

"But I've never been here before."

"Yes, you have. Clear your mind and breathe," Flora spoke in a quiet, calm voice. "Go back in your mind to when you were a little girl. You were walking along this same track. You were getting tired and wanted to be carried."

Jane stopped in her tracks. "Oh, my gosh! I was with Narana. She pulled some warrah down and tickled my face with it. It made me laugh."

"That's right." Flora agreed. "I saw that in the dream. Now, come this way please." Flora pushed past a large bush on the side of the path and walked into a small clearing. Honeysuckle in full bloom, was growing all around the sides of the clearing. The scent was overwhelming. Jane again felt a deep sorrow that seemed to rise from the depth of her soul.

"Close your eyes, Jane, and remember a long time ago when you were very little. Take yourself back farther. Remember." Flora was speaking so faintly that Jane could barely hear her.

Suddenly, Jane had the sensation she was sitting on someone's lap. She looked up and saw a young woman with long blonde hair and sad blue eyes.

"Just follow the thought, Jane. You can tell me where you are if you wish," Flora whispered.

"I'm sitting on her lap. She's blonde and looks like me. She seems so sad. I'm trying to play patty cake with her, but she's sleepy.... She's lying on the floor. I'm not with her anymore. Something's wrong. People are running and shouting. I'm sitting all alone. The smell ... it's the honeysuckle right beside me. I'm scared. I'm crying. I'm so alone. Why won't she wake up?" Jane rocked back and forth with her arms wrapped around herself. Tears were streaming down her face.

Flora put her arm around Jane and Jane buried her face in Flora's shoulder. "It was my mother. She died and I was sitting by the honeysuckle. That's why I've always cried."

"Stay there, Jane, and try to see what else is happening." Flora quickly encouraged Jane to keep going.

Jane took a deep, long breath, closed her eyes again and saw several Aboriginal men carrying someone toward her. "It's my father. He's sick. They're carrying him in the house and putting him in bed. Narana is trying to give him tea. He pushes her away. He's saying something. Oh! He won't take her medicine and my mother won't either. My God, that's why she died. She wouldn't go against his wishes. He told her not to take it. Narana could have saved them both, just like she saved herself. If only they would have taken her medicine!" Jane eyes flew open and she struggled to stand up. "Flora, could you see that? I saw it all. I was only a baby. My mother just blindly did what my father told her – and she died." Jane was shaking and Flora motioned for her to sit back down.

Jane and Flora stayed there in the midst of the honey-suckle for a while. Gradually, Jane relaxed and tried to sort through the significance of her uncovered memory. "I understand now why I cry when I smelled honeysuckle. And that I've been caught in the same trap as my mother. I've always done what I've been told to do by the men in my life, just like she did. But, that's all changed now, Flora. Why do I still feel so sad?"

"I think you've been trapped in the past, Jane. All your thoughts and behavior patterns were set one way and, even though you've struggled to change them, you haven't been able to let go of the past because you didn't understand it. Now you do. This experience will give you a new way to look at the world with wiser eyes. New choices are available to you now."

Jane and Flora strolled slowly back along the path. Jane felt extremely grateful to Flora for helping her have a special experience. She already felt a bit lighter at heart.

◎ ◎ ◎

When Jane returned to Lucy's house, glad to have a place to stay in Wainton, she wished Lucy and Michael still lived there. She felt lonely. She immediately went to the phone. She wanted, no, needed, to share her experience with someone. She called Fiona and relayed everything to her for nearly an hour. Fiona was equally impressed by Jane's experience, and fully agreed that it would help Jane release herself from the guilt that imprisoned her in the past. When Jane hung up, she still felt somewhat unsettled. She knew there was one more person she should share this information with – Charles.

Rather than call him, Jane decided to write him a letter. After describing her memory to Charles in detail and explaining her interpretation of its meaning, she thanked him for helping her grow up and for being her father. As she wrote, she felt very close to him. She expressed in the letter her wish to be closer to him. She did say she needed to do things her way, though she recognized that many of her attempts to be independent had been awkward at best. She concluded by saying how much she hoped this would be a turning point in their relationship. Jane reread her letter, decided it was exactly what she wanted to say, put a stamp on it and drove to the nearest post box so the letter would go out that very day. Later, she worried that perhaps she should have talked to Fiona about approaching Charles.

Reflecting ...

One day, when Jane returned to Lucy's, there was a beautiful bouquet of honeysuckle in a tin outside the front door. Flora must have brought it by, Jane guessed, smiling. She buried her nose in the fragrant blossoms and felt a sense of inner strength and oneness with nature. That's odd, she thought, in the past I've always cried and now I seem happy! It was as though the honeysuckle were the perfect tonic for letting go of the past. Jane carried it out to the veranda and placed it by her chair. She sat there for quite some time gazing at the trees and listening to the birds as they flew from tree to tree. It had been two days since the memory of her parents' deaths had come to her in the rainforest with Flora. She had been endlessly busy since that time. Now Jane felt a need to sit and contemplate the meaning of her memories or rather the meaning of her life.

Various conversations and experiences that she had shared with each of her teachers – as she had come to regard Flora, Fiona and Wong – had taught her that every event in life occurred for a reason. If she examined her life events closely enough, she would find her life purpose. Fiona had suggested that each of us decides before birth what our life purpose will be; it is one of our tasks in life to discover, or remember, that purpose. Moreover, every event in life is orchestrated to help us remember, if only we become aware of our search.

If this were so, then memories must contain important clues. Several things stood out to Jane. If her parents hadn't died, she would never have lived in the rainforest. Did her life purpose have something to do with the rainforest? Also, she had come to know Daraha and Flora and other Aboriginal people, which led her to develop a different outlook on life because of their mutual connection to Narana and the rainforest.

How did this all fit together? Jane's wealthy family seemed to be tied somehow together in this mystery. Her family's corporation was struggling now with negative press, but everyone, even Charles, was excited about the changes that were being made and the opportunities ahead. Somehow, she was getting closer to understanding. What was really important to her? Jane sat thinking about her needs and how they seemed to have changed. She had less need for a relationship with a man right now, but that was probably because she needed more time to get over Bob. Strangely enough, though, she didn't feel scared about being alone, although she was a bit lonely. After all her memories have come to life, she didn't have many fears, except maybe finding out that her family had done other terrible things just to make money.

A gentle breeze fluttered through the leaves of the nearby gum trees and Jane caught a whiff of the honeysuckle beside her. Intuitively, she sensed the honeysuckle was trying to communicate, and she began to breathe more slowly and deeply. A peace settled over her and her heart filled with joy. Jane realized that the honeysuckle had something to do with her feeling of well being ... and then she remembered, *plants!* Her life purpose was to study plants! She had been studying plants with Flora for sometime, but she hadn't realized the significance of it until now. She had wanted to study plants since her first camping trip, when she found the white root that tasted like licorice. She had wanted to study rainforest botany with Lucy at University. And then she had wanted to do post-graduate studies to discover new medicines that were made from plants. With all the other things that had happened, she had nearly forgotten her passions. Her thoughts were interrupted by loud screeching and a flock of sulphur-crested white cockatoos landed in the top of a nearby gum tree scaring away all the other birds for the moment. As Jane laughed at their antics, a thought crossed her mind. This was a significant moment.

The Birthday ...

Jane slept until dawn, opened her eyes and felt whole and refreshed. She lay in bed and luxuriated in stretching her legs and not feeling any pain. Her body felt alive, humming with joyous energy. The sky gradually lightened as she watched from her warm bed. She could hear birds chirping outside. A magpie warbled, then a second and third magpie joined in. Honeyeaters called to each other for several minutes, there was a cacophony of sound as though every bird alive were calling out joy as it greeted the sun.

She had come down to the city for the board meeting, believing that she was strong enough to take on more responsibilities. For a while, after the revelation at the refinery, Jane had been so weak that her family had encouraged her to stay in Wainton near the rainforest and just rest. She felt so much better now, she had even agreed to a small birthday dinner party Helen and Charles were throwing for her.

As Jane showered, it became clear to her that today, her twenty-fifth birthday, was a day with many reasons for celebrating. She smiled, acknowledging that Helen would never stop having parties for her. That was fine, it was going to be such a special day. First of all, she was going to the park for a picnic with Fiona, Lucy and Helen. Then she had to be at headquarters to sign all the papers. Jane felt elated as everything was going perfect – except perhaps her relationship with Charles. He hadn't mentioned her letter and she was afraid it might have angered him for some reason. Her relationship with him was the one area of her life that still was a puzzle. But she felt confident that it would all work out in time and, at least, Charles hadn't objected to her big plans.

Yes, her plans! At last Jane could see her ideas coming to life. She had been accepted into a post-graduate studies program starting next semester. Her supervisor assured her that she could concentrate her research on the medicinal plants of the rainforest. The next few months, before classes, would be spent in Wainton studying plants with Flora. Additionally, she would be starting another project close to her heart, the Lawton Foundation. The foundation had been Jane's idea and she was excited to be its first director. The purpose of the foundation was to provide grant monies for various kinds of Aboriginal-owned businesses. Funds came from the sale of stocks of two companies, which had only been partially owned by the corporation and whose stockholders did not agree with the new policies her family had established for the corporate holdings. The people at Lawton-Starr were sorry to lose their positive influence over the two companies, so establishing the Lawton Foundation seemed the perfect solution.

Jane dressed in a flowing skirt and a pretty blouse and decided to head out early to spend some time in the park alone before the others arrived, since it was such a beautiful morning. She drove down a sidetrack near the park and parked beside a clearing on the edge of the road. As she got out of the car, she could hear some kookaburras starting to laugh and she joined in, imitating their call quite badly. It was a glorious spring day; a day sent from heaven. The sky was a brilliant blue with fluffy, white clouds sailing across the heavens in slow motion. A breeze broke through the balmy air and gently lifted her skirt. Wildflowers were poking their heads up everywhere. Jane wandered through the meadow, running her hands softly over the tops of the young, growing grasses. They bent and swayed under her touch. On the hill ahead she could see an old gum tree with wide-spreading branches. When she reached it, she laid down on her back near its base, staring up at its limbs. The wind rustled through the leaves and several birds called from high up in the tree top. It was quite easy now, nearly automatic, for her to see the energy field around the tree and even the birds when they sat still. Jane could not remember ever feeling so awash in joy before.

She lay in a trance for a while, thinking of nothing and absorbing the warmth and light and sounds. As a breeze wafted around her cheek, she pondered whom else those molecules of air had touched; maybe her mother, Mary; maybe Narana, her beloved Aboriginal grandmother; or even maybe her great-great-grandmother, Joanna. She felt their energy encompassing her. The rustling of the leaves turned into whispering, *"Jane, we are with you."* She accepted the message comfortably as she was used to listening to more and more of them. She knew deep within herself that she had always heard them, but only recently did she start to listen instead of getting angry and ignoring them.

At the picnic with Lucy, Fiona and Helen – those who had been through so much with her – Jane raised her glass of bubbly pink lemonade, "To the future!"

In unison, they toasted her, "Happy Birthday, Jane. To the future!"

Lucy piped in, "To a future with lots of healthy plants and a healthy environment!"

Fiona contributed, "To a future where all people honor and celebrate their own and each others uniqueness."

After a brief hesitation, Helen took a deep breath, and offered, "Here's to a future where Charles and Jane learn to get along."

Jane looked sad for a moment and quietly said, "Yes, I'd like that." Then, raising her head, she changed her tone, "Now, it's my party, and I get the final say!"

Everyone nodded her support, and sat silent for a moment. A sunbeam broke through a cloud at that moment and illuminated the group. Everyone grinned simultaneously, and Jane commented, "How appropriate! Here's to a future when the earth and all living things live in balance and harmony."

The intimate, little group broke into delighted applause, hugging each other and dancing around the clearing. Jane was not at all surprised when her comic bird friends joined in the cheer from the branches above. Leave it to the kookaburras, they always laughed at the appropriate moment.

The Gift ...

As she drove to her parents' house after leaving headquarters, she began to feel a bit nervous. Here she was a grown woman and she felt edgy just because Charles had asked if he could talk with her privately before her birthday dinner party. She feared his demands; he always wanted to control what she did and said. Jane pulled over and stopped on the side of the road, took a few deep breaths, sent some energy through her body and started to feel much calmer. She recognized that her childhood feelings were taking over again. She smiled bravely and reminded herself of what

Lucy often said, she was running this body's thoughts and emotions, no one else. "Right!" she said out loud to herself. She pulled back into traffic and flipped the radio on.

As she walked up the pathway to her parents' house, Charles came out the front door. She felt shy and oddly unsure what to say. She could tell he felt the same.

"Jane, I'm glad to see you," he said, following her inside and ushering her into the study.

Jane paused in the doorway, "Dad, do you mind if we sit in the sunroom? This room holds bad memories for me."

Charles looked at her quietly, "No, that is fine, Jane."

As they walked to the sunroom, Charles began talking, "Jane, what you said in your letter to me, reminded me of what I have been thinking about a lot." They entered the sunroom and took chairs opposite each other. "I know you have been researching the family history lately. And, well, that chest you asked me for, I want you to have it. Last year, when you asked for it, I got angry and couldn't really explain why. But I wasn't angry at you Jane, I realized that later, I was angry at life. That chest was your mother's, Mary's, I mean." He covered his face to hide his emotions

"Jane, it broke my heart when she died. We were so close, especially when we were children. Our grandmother gave that chest to Mary and, according to her, it came across on the boat from England with Joanna, her mother when she was a little girl. The chest was washed upon shore after the shipwreck, and the Aborigines made sure that little Joanna got it back. Evidently, one of the Aborigines had taken a special liking to Joanna and for a fact, had probably saved her life. That chest holds so many special memories! Oh, I've always intended for you to inherit it when I die. It's just that when you asked for it, I felt in a way that you were treating me as though I were already dead, and that hurt me a lot." Charles looked up at her with a distorted grin. Jane took his hands in hers.

"Oh, Dad! I'm so sorry, I came across so harshly back then. I really appreciate your giving the chest to me. Even though I don't always agree with you,..." she smiled ruefully and they both let out a sheepish laugh, "I do love you. I very much want you to be happy with my choices."

Her father listened and then stood up abruptly and cleared his throat, and said, "You do seem to be happier now, Jane. I'm glad about that. Well, that's it then. The blanket chest is your birthday gift from me. Would you like it sent up to Wainton?"

"Yes, that would be great. Thank you! I'm going to rent Lucy and Michael's house, since they don't want to sell it yet." Jane stepped closer to Charles, reached up and gave him a kiss on the cheek. "Thank you," she whispered softly.

The Blanket Chest ...

Two weeks later, after Jane had returned to Wainton and was getting settled, transforming Lucy's house into her home, the blanket chest arrived. Jane put it in the bedroom. It seemed to belong there. As she sat up in bed writing that evening, she kept glancing at it, feeling comforted by its presence. She could remember opening it up when she was about ten, and dressing up in the old clothes she found inside. She hadn't realized then how old the blanket chest was. Now it connected her to her past and gave her a sense of her family heritage which had taken a new importance in her life. Jane drifted off to sleep that night wondering what life had been like in her great-great-grandmother's time.

> *The ship is tossing side to side. There is water everywhere. She is slipping, a wave engulfs her. She sees her body slam into the ship rail and wash overboard. Total blackness embraces her. A warm safe, feeling replaces panic as fear gives way to love. She feels a tapping on her forehead. A black face appears in front of her, and a familiar voice says: "Open this and see, you've been here before. You were beautiful then, you are beautiful now. The secret lies in knowing."*

Jane became aware of the kookaburras laughing in the trees outside her window. She cracked open her eyes, and saw that it was it was beginning to get light. She rolled her head to one side as she stretched and saw a hazy image of the blanket chest sitting across the room. She remembered helping her mother pack the chest for a long voyage. She was so excited. Her father was taking them on his ship to a new home. Then she realized she wasn't asleep. Jane took a deep breath and tried to process what was happening. Words from her dream came back to her. Had she actually been there? Had *she* been Joanna? She felt a sharp searing pain in her hip making her cry out. It felt like it was broken! Oh, my God! she thought as the significance of it swept over her. Her arthritis was the memory of the broken hip from the shipwreck. She had lost her mother then too. Jane began to sweat. She tried to sit up in bed, but fell back, her head spinning dizzily. She curled up tight in a little ball.

It was late morning; the hot sun shining in the window, came to rest on Jane's face and woke her up. She was curled up in a ball again. Jane stretched and felt the pain in her hip. The arthritis had been scarcely noticeable since that day in the rainforest with Flora when she remembered her parents' death. Now it was back full force. Jane began her breathing meditation. She watched her breath as it flowed in through her feet and progressed up through all her joints, up to her forehead and then back down again. Over and over, slowly, rhythmically she breathed. Gradually the hip relaxed until at last she could straighten her legs. The pain in her left hip had always been much more severe than in her right. Now she knew why. Joanna's left hip had been broken. Jane gasped sharply. She knew she was Joanna and now she is Jane. It all connected and she remembered everything. Joanna and Jane had lost their mothers. A wonderful loving black woman had rescued both of them. Both had pain in their left hip. The synchronicity was too overwhelming. Jane had to talk to someone. She sat up, slid to the head of the bed and reached for the phone.

"Aunt Fiona!" She nearly shouted into the receiver. "I must talk to you right away. You'll never believe what has happened. I remember...."

Fiona cut in, "Jane, just a moment. I'm sorry, but I have an important meeting in five minutes and I need to prepare. I can call you back this evening. Will you be home?"

"Oh, sure," Jane felt deflated. "I think I can wait that long." Jane replaced the phone and started to slide out of bed, but she was slowed down by the pain in her hip. She stood up, carefully stretched, and slowly made her way to the shower. She wondered if her newly uncovered memory would make her arthritis worse, or if maybe it was the key to her getting well now?

While she showered, Jane concluded that she could use more information on her family history, and would do some research at the library. That way, when she talked to Fiona later, she might have some verification for her experience.

The Family History...

Jane sighed as she shut the heavy volume she had been skimming. She had been in the library for four hours straight and she needed some sun. Her notebook was crammed with information, and she felt she had achieved as much as she could for now. She decided to call it a day.

Jane picked up a sandwich and coffee and wandered over to sit in the park. Her mind was still mulling over what she had read. It was recorded that a ship named *Joanna* had shipwrecked off the coast of Victoria, at a place now called Johanna. The reports of the shipwreck were varied, with some saying that everyone survived and others saying that not all recovered. It was clear there were some Aborigines in the area, but only one report mentioned them helping the survivors. At least all the reports agreed that the captain's name was Captain Johnson, from Plymouth England, and that he was emigrating with his wife and daughter to Australia. One report even noted that he eventually returned and settled the land where the ship was wrecked, claiming the bush for a sheep farm and clearing it all by hand. Captain Johnson must be her great- great-great-grandfather, or something like that. He was her mother's grandmother's grandfather.

That evening, Jane sat in bed looking at the blanket chest. She had a curious feeling about it, so she got up and knelt beside it. She ran her fingers over the inner lining of the lid and felt a bulge back near the hinges. She got a knife from the kitchen and split open the lining, gasping, when an old black notebook tumbled out. With trembling hands, Jane opened it to reveal lines of spidery handwriting. The first line in the book read, *"I, Captain Johnson do solemnly declare..."* She closed it and stood up. This was too much. Still quivering, she managed to call Flora, who promised to come over straight away. Jane was waiting for her with a pot of tea when she arrived. After Jane showed Flora the blanket chest in her bedroom; they sat down at the kitchen table beside the open window and read from the old notebook.

It turned out to be a journal filled mostly with entries about weather, farming, crops, droughts and the hardships of living in a foreign land. Towards the end, it became obvious why Captain Johnson had hidden the journal. He wrote briefly that he had met a native girl and planned to marry her. He made no mention of Joanna until near the end, where he said that Joanna and her husband seemed pleased that he was remarrying after all these years. His entries weren't dated, but it appeared that it was started after Joanna had left home to get married. Following his entry about marrying the native girl, there was only one more. Captain Johnson wrote that he hoped the family of his native bride would come to live on his land, where there would be enough food for all of them. He added that he was afraid the local white community would not be pleased with his choices. He ended by saying that he would hide this diary and write more later. But, there were no more entries.

"Flora, that's not all I discovered. Last night, after I moved the blanket chest into the bedroom, I had a dream. I dreamt about the shipwreck and it was as though I were really there! Then, later when I was half awake, I remember thinking that I was Joanna. I had her thoughts and memories. I remembered the Aboriginal woman who saved her and that her hip had been broken. It was as though it were the same pain that I have now in my left hip. Do you think that is possible?"

"You mean reincarnation?" Flora asked and Jane nodded. "Well," Flora mused, "I'm not sure if I exactly understand the concept of reincarnation, but I do believe we contain the memories of our ancestors, and perhaps those memories are actually stored in our bodies. Maybe that is what science means by genetics?... I don't know. Have you talked to Fiona?"

Before Jane could answer, the phone rang, and Jane broke out in a laugh. "That's her now!"

Flora went out on the veranda while Jane shared her news with Fiona over the phone. Flora pondered whether it really was true that we have all lived before in different bodies. It certainly would explain away a lot of questions.

Jane came out and joined her after awhile. "Fiona says that such an experience does suggest reincarnation and that I am remembering a past life. The concept is a bit more than I bargained for you know, but it is fascinating. Fiona thought there may be more under the surface, and that I must understand how it relates to my life in the present."

Jane and Flora exchanged glances. Then Jane thought of something that had been puzzling her. "The strange thing is Flora, I got the impression that Joanna's father disliked the Aborigines. And I thought he wouldn't let the Aboriginal woman who had saved her life be near her. My feeling is that Joanna was extremely lonely and unhappy. Maybe her father softened in his old age and changed his attitude toward Aborigines, do you think?"

"There is no way to know, my child. I'm so tired now, and think I must go and get some sleep."

"Oh, please stay here! There is another bedroom all set up for guests. I'd feel better if you could stay, just this once."

Flora agreed. She could see that Jane was a little disturbed by all that had happened. Jane showed Flora to the guest room, and went back into her bedroom and was closing the lid to the chest, when a sheet fluttered out of the cut in the lining. The paper was yellowed and cracked, and the writing was faded. It was a letter addressed to Captain William Johnson.

"Dear William
We were pleased to get your letter and hope that this reaches you in good health. I must say that we were both horrified to learn about your neighbor poisoning the natives. We have heard that they are primitives but this is extremely evil to treat any human being in this way. We understand how very shocked you must be by this incident and wish you well in trying to recover some form of . . . ."

The letter went on but Jane could read no further, tears were blurring her vision. She had read at the library about the Aborigines being poisoned and it made her sick to her stomach to learn that they had been treated so inhumanely. She knew she had avoided thinking more about it; perhaps she was afraid of coming across evidence that her ancestor had been involved in the poisonings. But according to the letter, Captain Johnson was not involved.

Flora appeared in the doorway in her nightdress and quietly took the letter from Jane's hand. She skimmed it and then looked at Jane's face. Flora spoke reassuringly, "I knew you were worried about the poisonings and that you couldn't mention it to me. I'm sure your ancestor wasn't involved. But you know, we are all still healing from what happened so long ago. I am, you are, everyone is. As we remember and heal, the Aboriginal spirits who have been tied to those tragic places for such a long time are being freed and return to the great Creator."

"Oh, my..." Jane was overcome by a sudden feeling of knowing. "The same events were played out here at the sugar refinery. My family was taking land away from the Aboriginal people and tragedy resulted. How can this cycle ever be stopped?" Jane collapsed on her bed and drew up into a tight little ball.

Flora came over and put her hand on Jane's hip. "You're stopping it my child. That's why you're remembering. The work you and your family are doing in this life is changing the tide and moving us all toward a new balance and harmony. Now straighten out your legs and breathe. You don't have to hold that pain any longer. Release it now."

Jane looked up at Flora's eyes as she slowly straightened out. She inhaled deeply and sat up. As she did, Jane felt a huge weight suddenly lift off of her body and she experienced a wonderful sense of lightness and freedom. The air around her suddenly sparkled as though it were effervescent and Jane was filled with joy. Flora was gazing upward and smiling peacefully, tears running down her cheeks.

The Future ...

Jane was up early the next morning and watched the lightening of the sky from her window, listening to the cackling laughter of the kookaburras. She spotted a beautiful white cockatoo perched on a branch of a tree just outside her window. It seemed to be beckoning Jane to come outside. She quickly got up, dressed and hurried out, leaving a short note for Flora. "Beach" was all she needed to say.

Sunrise was brilliant; all the colours of the rainbow were visible: red, orange, yellow, green, blue, magenta and the most beautiful shade of purple. Jane lay on the sand watching the sky's colours melt into the water. The same colours rippled on the backs of the waves, as they rushed toward her. Gradually, the sun rose over the horizon and Jane knew she would never be alone again.

About the Authors

Cinda Wombles Pettigrew, RN, MIICA, is an cncrgy consultant, spiritual counselor and teacher who assists others to consciously live their spirituality. Cinda and her husband, Jim, travel to many countries which affords her the opportunity to explore the deep spiritual and cultural heritage of the native people. When not traveling and writing, she enjoys tennis, boating on the Mississippi River and walking in the forest which surrounds their home.

ⓖ ⓖ ⓖ

Born in Australia, Robyn D. Warncr is one of six sisters and holds a Ph.D. in food science from the University of Wisconsin. She is a research scientist at the Victorian Institute for Animal Science. Robyn's love of nature frequently leads to adventures in the Australian outback with her geographer husband, Peter. She enjoys spending her leisure time bird watching, bushwalking, and camping in the wilderness.